MW01128685

Bookstore at Holiday Bay:

Once Upon a Mystery

by

Kathi Daley

The Bookstore at Holiday Bay

Once upon a Mystery

Once Upon a Haunting

The Inn at Holiday Bay

The Bistro at Holiday Bay

Opera and Old Lace

Moonlight and Broomsticks

Cupid and Cool Jazz

Sunshine and Sweet Wine

Chapter 1

I bought a bookstore.

It's not as if I'd planned to make this huge purchase at this point in my life. In fact, if you'd told me a year ago that shortly after my sixty-second birthday, Louise Prescott, Lou to most, would move halfway across the country to a new home, new business, and new community of friends and neighbors, I'd have said you were crazy. Of course, if you'd likewise told me a year ago that I was destined to become a widow at the ripe young age of sixty-one, I might have realized that sometimes the need for change isn't so much about the crazy as it is about the grief.

"I think we should move the coffee counter to the open space along that back wall so the area near the picture window can be used for seating," I said to my new business partner, Velma Crawford. Velma had recently lost the business she'd loved and nurtured in a fire, bringing her a different type of grief. Velma's grief, as mine had for me, had prompted changes I was sure she'd never seen coming. Rather than rebuilding the diner where she'd spent so much of her life up to this point, she'd accepted the buyout her insurance company offered, married her live-in partner, Royce Crawford, bought a motor home, and headed out on a journey across the country. When the happy couple returned to Holiday Bay after nearly two months away, Velma decided it was time to go back to work. She'd heard I was looking to take on a partner interested in opening a coffee and pastry bar inside the bookstore, and the rest, as they say, was fate.

"I agree," Velma said. "It'd be ideal if folks could settle in with a good book, an excellent cup of coffee, and an unbeatable view. I've been thinking that perhaps we should consider adding a gas fireplace or stove in the corner on the far side of the picture window. Doing so would create a cozy setting on a snowy winter day."

I glanced toward the large picture window that looked out over the bay. It was a sunny day today, with temperatures climbing into the mid-seventies, but I could imagine the snowy scene Velma seemed to be describing. "I like that concept. In fact, I love most of the ideas we've come up with, including the proposal for a cat rescue right here in the bookstore."

Velma chuckled. "I was wondering how long it was going to take for Hazel to convince you of the wisdom of her plan."

I smiled. "Initially, when Hazel suggested that we have a designated area where cats from the local rescue could be showcased, I wasn't sure how the idea would work in the real world. I've done my research, however, and I think that as long as we maintain both a cat-friendly area for those who want to mingle with our feline friends and a cat-free zone for those who are allergic or prefer not to be bothered, we'll be fine."

I picked up the orange rescue kitten Hazel Hawthorn had dropped off at the bookstore a few days ago. At the time, she'd assured me that she only needed me to watch the kitten for a few hours while she rounded up a foster home. I'd been reluctant to commit, but I'd agreed after a small amount of persuasion on Hazel's part. Of course, that was three days ago, and I still had the kitten. Velma, who'd known Hazel a lot longer than I had, apologetically informed me that it was unlikely that the cat woman of Holiday Bay had ever planned to come back for him.

Not that I minded. Not really. Lou Prescott was no pushover, and the fact that Hazel had pulled a fast one on me should have had me steaming from the ears. But Velma assured me that Hazel was a sensitive woman who likely realized that I needed the kitten as much as he needed me and decided to take matters into her own hands by getting the two of us together.

"So what do you think, little guy?" I held the kitten up and looked him in the eye. "Should we commit to having a cat rescue in the bookstore?"

The kitten batted me on the nose and then struggled to get down. He was the independent sort who I could already see wasn't going to want to spend a lot of time cuddled up on my lap. Some people might find this to be a negative, but I was a busy woman, so I was okay with a kitten who was as self-reliant as I was.

"Perhaps we can build a separate lounge where the cats can hang out," Velma suggested. "I'm not sure how that would look exactly, but this is a large space with quite a few rooms and closets that, to this point, have been used for storage. If we move things around a bit, perhaps we can make it work."

"I think we can," I agreed as I set the kitten on the floor. "I guess I should name the little guy if he's going to be a permanent resident."

"I've always been fond of Toby," Velma suggested.

I rolled the name around in my mind. "Toby. I like it." I glanced at the kitten. "So what do you think? Does Toby work for you?"

The kitten totally ignored me, which wasn't really surprising. I didn't suppose Toby cared what his name was going to be. I sent him a look intended as a welcome, and then I turned and glanced at the clock. "The women for the Tuesday night book club meeting will arrive soon." The Tuesday night book club was a group of mystery-loving women who seemed more interested in discussing current events than the book of the week.

"I ran into Hazel yesterday, and she shared her plan to invite Gwen Harbinger," Velma informed me.

"I'm not sure I've met Gwen yet."

"She's a nice woman. I guess she's around our age, maybe a few years younger. Gwen recently lost her husband."

"I'm sorry to hear that."

"Young man, too," Velma continued. "I don't know his exact age, but I'm guessing he was in his late fifties or early sixties." She paused. "He worked a fishing boat in the area for years. Big guy. Seemed like the invincible sort." She made a sound that sounded like a snort. "In the end, I guess none of us are as invincible as we'd like to believe."

I smiled. "Oh, I don't know. I feel pretty invincible." I glanced at the reflection of the petite woman with long white hair in the large picture window. "Well, maybe not as invincible as I once was," I altered my statement as I considered the changes that had taken place in the past few years.

Velma laughed. "I get it. I was standing in my pretty little bathroom, brushing my teeth a few weeks ago, and it suddenly hit me that I no longer recognized the woman in the mirror staring back at me." She touched a hand to her short gray hair. "Not that there's anything wrong with the woman I've become; in fact, I like her just fine, but it was somewhat unsettling to suddenly realize that I just don't look like me anymore."

"I get it," I said. "I've had the same experience in the past where I just stand in my bathroom staring at the white-haired woman in the mirror and wondering about the dark-haired girl I'd once been."

"It's a sobering experience," Velma agreed. "The reality is that the change to our bodies, like many of the other changes in our lives, is a slow process that sneaks up on us as the years fade one into another." She paused and then continued. "I know there are those who spend a lot of money to fight the natural progression of things, but it seems to me that accepting these changes with courage and grace is the real key to happiness as our lives evolve. And I'm not just talking about the physical changes such as weight gain and gray hair. I'm talking about larger life changes as well." Her voice grew soft. "For me, it was losing the diner. I guess I never realized how much my sense of self was all wrapped up in that building and that business. Not until I lost it, that is. After the fire, I knew there would be financial fallout to consider, but I truly didn't understand the emotional toll this major change in my life would have on me."

Given the dramatic changes that my life had undergone after my husband's death, I knew just how true that statement was. A year ago, I was living my perfect life. Perfect husband, perfect home, and perfect community of friends and neighbors. Not only was I about as happy as a sixty-one-year-old retiree can be, but I was motivated and enthusiastic for the future I'd been working toward. And then, in the blink of an eye, the man I planned to live out my life with died. It hadn't been expected. He hadn't been sick or frail. He hadn't suffered symptoms of any sort before the heart attack that took his life. With Gus's death, my happy life dissolved in front of me. I'd been in shock for so long that I'd barely noticed the passage of time, but once I had returned to the living, I found that all I had left were the ashes of what could have been, what should have been, and what would never be.

"Do we have snacks for the meeting?" I asked, shaking off the melancholy I felt seeping into my veins.

"Marnie and Cricket volunteered to bring pastries, so all we need to provide tonight is coffee. I'll make a pot now." Velma offered.

Marnie and Cricket Abernathy were sisters who'd moved to Holiday Bay from the south this past fall. They'd opened a flower shop named All About Bluebells and seemed to be doing quite well for themselves. Marnie was a voracious reader and often voiced her opinion that our group might actually want to discuss the book we'd all agreed to read, but Cricket was all about the gossip. Even though I'd purchased the bookstore on the bay from my niece, Vanessa Blackstone, I had to admit that deep down inside, I sided with Cricket. As far as I was concerned, the best part about the Tuesday night book club meetings wasn't the books but the kinship and the conversation.

"I'll head into the backroom to set up the chairs," I offered while Velma made the coffee.

After retrieving twelve chairs from one of the storage closets, I neatly arranged them in a circle. As I prepared the room for our book club meeting, I thought about the women who would fill those chairs. Velma and I would take seats on opposite sides of the large circle. Neither of us was a huge reader, which was interesting given our current status as bookstore owners, but we liked to appear engaged and involved for those club members, such as Marnie, who really were here to discuss the book.

Marnie and Cricket generally sat to my left. It wasn't as if we had assigned seating, but the southern sisters tended to show up a good twenty minutes before anyone else, and since, as the first to arrive, they had their choice of seats, I could understand why they'd choose chairs that looked toward the window with a view of the bay. If the conversation lagged, at least there was something to look at.

I enjoyed my relationship with Marnie and Cricket. Even though I was a good thirty years older than the lively pair, we originally hailed from the same part of South Carolina, which created a bond that might not otherwise have existed. Not that we'd all lived in South Carolina at the same time since I'd married and moved to Northern Minnesota before either sister had even been born, but the bond that was forged by a common history and tradition made us sisters of the most important kind.

I stood back and looked at my circle of chairs. Bonnie Singleton had mentioned that she might bring a guest this evening. Gabby Gibson was the new dispatcher assigned to the Holiday Bay Police Department. I'd previously met her and was anxious to deepen that relationship, so I hoped it would work out for her to attend.

Bonnie's sister, Beverly Singleton, had likewise invited a guest to the group. Alice Farthington was a recently widowed kindergarten teacher from the local elementary school. She was only twenty-eight, which, in my opinion, was much too young to be a widow. Everyone seemed to agree that fate had been unfair to this young woman who'd suffered the loss of her mate so early in life. Of course, I'd learned long ago that fate didn't seem to care about what was right or wrong, fair or unfair. Fate simply was.

I liked to think I've mostly learned to live with my own grief. Most of the time, those around me aren't even aware of the hole in my chest where my heart used to live. People say that I'm strong. They say that I'm brave. They say they admire how I've been able to move on, but the truth of the matter is that the face I show to the world is a lie, and beneath that façade is a broken woman who is simply trying to get through each moment as it fades into the next.

After a bit of consideration, I decided to add two additional hardwood folding chairs to the mix. Not that we'd necessarily need them, but it was good to have them just in case our part-timers all decided to attend. Shelby Morris only showed up about fifty percent of the time. She loved to gossip and tried to make it when she could, but she had a restaurant to run, and while Tuesday evenings generally weren't busy, allowing her to get away, there were weeks when she needed to be at the Bistro at Holiday Bay to oversee things.

Georgia Carter was another part-timer. She helped run the Inn at Holiday Bay that Abby Sullivan owned and often got held up when things were busy. I enjoyed spending time with Georgia when she made it to the meeting. She was a hoot and a half and seemed to keep everyone laughing. Georgia was responsible for several new recruits, including Emma Brown, a recent widow after nearly fifty years of marriage. Emma had moved to Holiday Bay after meeting a man named Joel Stafford. Joel was a retired history professor and would make an excellent addition to our book group, although so far, the group was comprised entirely of women. Single women, I clarified as it occurred to me that every woman in our group, with the exception of Velma, was either widowed or had never married.

Once the chairs were arranged, I headed back toward the front of the bookstore, where I could hear Velma chatting with Cricket. Marnie was arranging a platter of pastries which were both colorful and delicious looking, while Velma and Cricket discussed the changes that had been taking place in the community. After Velma's Diner burned, Velma sold the land to a developer who sold the land to a man who wanted to open a brewery. The brewery would require a much larger space than the diner had occupied, so the developer needed to buy the businesses on either side of the diner. The dress shop had been relocated, and the secondhand jewelry and electronics store had closed. Both buildings had been torn down, and construction of the brewery had already begun.

In addition to the brewery, other new businesses were sprouting up around town. Desperate for Donuts was now a pizza parlor with the best thin-crust pies I'd ever eaten, and the curio shop on the corner now housed a psychic, who most folks seemed to think was the real thing.

"I really am grateful to Shelby for hiring all my displaced help," Velma was saying to Cricket as I walked up behind them. "Knowing that my staff is being taken care of has given me peace of mind."

Cricket reached for a cup of freshly brewed coffee. "I know you're grateful to Shelby, but everyone knows you did Shelby a favor by sending your displaced employees to talk to her. The Bistro has been slammed all summer. That new rooftop seating area is the hottest hot spot that Holiday Bay has seen in a very long time. Most days, there's a waiting list to get a seat up there."

"The view from the rooftop is pretty great," I agreed. "Velma and I went up for a late dinner and a drink last week, and we simply couldn't get over how perfect it was to listen to the waves below while looking up into the starry sky."

"Shelby told me that they'd planned to have live music on the roof during July and August, but it's been so crowded that she's thinking they might just skip it," Velma informed us.

"The music they had playing over the stereo system was nice and not as loud as live music would be. It'd be a shame to drown out the sound of the waves," I added, looking up from my conversation with Cricket as Georgia walked in with Emma. I smiled and gave the women a wave just a split second before Bonnie and Beverly Singleton wandered in with Gabby Gibson and Alice Farthington. Changing course, I headed in their direction. I tried to speak to each individual who attended a book club meeting, but that didn't always work out. This week, I felt that if I needed to choose, it really did seem the most important to greet Holiday Bay's most recent widow as well as Holiday Bay's most recent resident.

"Gabby, Alice." I smiled, reaching out to touch each woman briefly on the arm. "I'm so happy the two of you could make it."

"I've been trying to get out and meet everyone since I've been here," Gabby said. "It's been a challenge with Colt keeping me so busy, but I'm doing a fair job so far." She referred to Police Chief Colt Wilder as she looked around the room. "Looks like a fair number of folks are here whom I haven't met yet."

Bonnie took her arm. "I'll take you around and introduce you."

Beverly had wandered off as well, leaving me alone with Alice.

"So I understand you teach kindergarten at the local elementary school."

She nodded. It appeared the girl was shy, or perhaps she felt overwhelmed after allowing Beverly to railroad her into attending tonight.

"I know this group is a lot to take in." I took her hand. "Come with me. I'm going to introduce you to Marnie Abernathy. Have you met Marnie?"

"I know who she is, but I haven't met her. Although I do know Shelby, the woman she's talking to."

"That's perfect. I'll introduce you to Marnie, and then the three of you can chat until we begin."

"Will you begin soon?" she asked.

I looked at the clock on the wall. Technically, we should have started fifteen minutes ago, but we liked to wait for everyone to arrive. The only two who hadn't yet arrived were Hazel and Gwen. Perhaps they had become involved in a discussion concerning Gwen's recent loss after Hazel stopped by her home to pick her up. That would be understandable. I remembered those first months after my Gus died. I was such a mess that my friends had been afraid to visit for fear of saying the wrong thing or, even worse, not having anything to say. But the reality was that there was nothing anyone could have said to make the situation either harder or easier to handle. I'd lost the love of my life, and the only thing that would ever ease my pain was the long slow journey through the middle of it.

"It looks like we're missing two members," I said to Alice, "but I think I'm going to go ahead and suggest we retire to the backroom where the chairs are set up. I'll walk you over to Shelby and introduce you to Marnie before I start rounding everyone up."

As I'd predicted, Marnie and Alice got along fabulously. The women both had a thoughtful and responsible side and tended to be more introverted than extroverted. Marnie and Alice appeared to have merged into a lively discussion of books they'd both read in the past, which sent Shelby across the room to a corner where Georgia and Emma were chatting with Velma and Gabby.

"Have you heard from either Hazel or Gwen?" I asked Velma after heading toward the corner where she was holding court.

"No. Not since this afternoon when Hazel called to let me know that Gwen had agreed to come this evening. I hope they're okay."

"It seems likely Gwen needed to talk when Hazel arrived to pick her up. I remember times after Gus passed away when a mood would hit me just right, and I cornered one of my unsuspecting friends. I suspect they'll wander in later. I'm going to go ahead and start ushering everyone into the backroom."

"That's a good idea," Velma agreed. "I'll grab the coffee pot and head in that direction."

As it turned out, neither Hazel nor Gwen had shown up that evening. Everyone in attendance seemed to have a wonderful time. Marnie seemed grateful that, as she had, Alice, Emma, and Gabby had actually read the book we'd gathered to discuss. Georgia had likewise read the book in its entirety, and the Singleton sisters had each read half the book, making for a fairly lively discussion. The book we'd read for this week's book club meeting was a mystery with lots of twists and turns that I really enjoyed. Next week, our selection was a widely held romance with a touch of suspense.

"I'm going to call Hazel and find out what happened," I said after the meeting broke up, and almost everyone began tidying up the room and putting chairs away.

"Don't bother," Gabby said, taking her cell phone out of her purse for the first time since turning it off once the book discussion had begun. "I have a message from Alex." She looked up and looked me in the eye. "Gwen Harbinger has been found dead."

Chapter 2

Poor Hazel had found Gwen sitting in her car when she'd stopped by her home to pick her up for the book club meeting. It appeared that the grief of losing her spouse had been too much for the woman who was found inside an enclosed garage with her car's engine running.

Almost everyone I'd spoken to since hearing the news of Gwen's passing agreed that the recent widow had been struggling to cope. Most understood that for someone in so much pain, suicide might have seemed to have been a viable option.

Everyone other than Hazel, that is. Hazel knew Gwen better than most, and despite what looked to be a cut-and-dried cause of death, Hazel insisted that Gwen would never have put her adult children through the loss of a second parent so soon after the first. In her mind, death by suicide was out of the question. Initially, I wasn't sure that I agreed with Hazel. The memory of my anger and fear when Gus passed away unexpectedly was still fresh in my mind, as was the feeling of emptiness that felt too huge to bear once I really let it sink in that he was never coming home.

"It seems obvious to me that Alex is going to need our help if she's going to solve this case," Hazel said to Velma and me as the three of us, along with my kitten, Toby, sat around a long table enjoying the early morning sunshine as it streamed in through the window. Colt had taken his niece and nephew to visit relatives on their father's side of the family and had left his new recruit, Officer Alex Weston, in charge. Alex appeared to be an excellent cop with good instincts, but since she'd only been on the job for a short time, she didn't know the local players the way Colt did.

"I understand that this is a difficult and heartbreaking situation," Velma responded, "but I'm not sure there's a case to solve. Based on everything I've learned to date, I have to agree that it looks as if Gwen was overwhelmed by her loss and simply decided to end her suffering."

"She wouldn't do that," Hazel argued.

Velma sent Hazel a gentle look. "Maybe not, but even if Gwen didn't intentionally end her life and something else actually occurred, I'm sure Alex is capable of figuring out what happened."

Hazel narrowed her gaze before responding. "I don't disagree that Alex is an extremely competent and capable young woman, but you and I know a lot more about the local players than Alex will be able to sort through, given the limited amount of time she's had in the community."

"Have you discussed the situation with Alex?" I asked Hazel.

"Actually, I have," Hazel answered. "She agrees with me that something feels off, but she also feels stuck to find an explanation other than suicide since there's absolutely zero evidence that Gwen didn't simply end her own life as it appears that she did."

"Alex didn't find anything at all?" Velma asked. "Fingerprints that didn't belong at the scene or random hairs or fibers."

"As far as I know, Alex found nothing unusual at the scene," Hazel stated again. "I know how this looks. A woman who has been deeply grieving the loss of her soulmate turns up dead in her car inside her garage, and every piece of evidence that exists, or in this case, doesn't exist, points to suicide, but I'm telling you that Gwen wouldn't end her own life. The Gwen I knew would deal with her grief and move on with her life. There has to be something else going on."

I decided to take a back seat in the conversation and simply allow Velma and Hazel to work it out. I was new to town and didn't have the history, so I didn't feel it was my place to voice an opinion.

"Okay. So what exactly are you proposing?" Velma asked Hazel after the conversation lulled.

"I'm proposing that the three of us help Alex with the investigation," Hazel said. "Alex doesn't appear to be the territorial sort, and my impression when I spoke to her was that she was simply after the truth, whatever that might be."

"Colt has always been that way as well," Velma pointed out. "If he wasn't faced with a difficult situation relating to his dead sister's children, I know he'd be right beside us looking for the truth." It was obvious that it was important to her that the man who was like a son to her didn't come off looking bad due to the fact that he wasn't in town to stick up for himself.

"I'm not blaming Colt," Hazel said. "He's been put in a tough situation, and I know that he's doing the best that he can, but his attention is divided. I asked Alex if the county would send a temp to help while Colt was away, and she said no. Alex is a great kid, but she's only one person. As I've said on numerous occasions, she will need help."

"Who's going to need help?" Cricket asked as she and Marnie filed into the bookstore from the sidewalk.

"We were talking about the fact that Alex has been left alone as the only law enforcement personnel on staff while Colt is out of town," Hazel said.

"Oh." Cricket nodded. "It is true that Alex has been left to deal with the situation on her own. I spoke to her this morning, and she assured me that she's more than capable of investigating Gwen's death, but I can assure you that she will need help sorting through the various residents that might need to be spoken to."

"Do you think she will?" Hazel asked. "Interview folks that may have known the couple."

"I think she will to the extent that she has time," Cricket said. "Alex is a real go-getter, but she's been handed a lot, so I think we should all be realistic about what is fair to expect from her."

"I agree that she may need help, but before we get too far into this, maybe we should invite Alex over and hear what she has to say," I said.

"I agree with that," Velma seconded.

"I'll call her right now," Hazel offered. She looked at me. "Can I use the phone in your office? My cell phone is dead."

"Yes, of course, you can. You know where it is."

After she left, Velma asked those of us who remained if we really thought that our getting involved in Alex's case while Colt was away was the best idea.

"I think it is," I spoke up.

"Me too," Cricket agreed.

Velma looked at Marnie. Marnie answered. "As long as we're upfront with Alex and keep her in the loop at all times, I think it would be a good idea for us to poke around a bit. I didn't know Gwen. At least I didn't know her well. But Hazel did, and she seems convinced that suicide was not a factor despite Alex's first take on things."

Hazel returned from the office with news that Alex was tied up this morning but would be happy to speak to us once she got freed up. Alex suggested she come by the bookstore around lunchtime, and Hazel agreed to return around noon.

I looked at Marnie and Cricket. "Can the two of you make it back?"

"We can," Marnie assured me. "Cricket and I need to get back to the flower shop since we have a half dozen deliveries to make, but before we go, we wanted to talk to you about the reason we came by in the first place."

"Our lowlife, pond-scum, algae-sucking, bottom-feeding landlord canceled our lease," Cricket said before Marnie could complete her thought.

"He canceled your lease?" I asked.

Dark-haired Marnie nodded, her bright blue eyes flashing with annoyance. "The man had us served with a thirty-day notice to vacate the property when we arrived at the flower shop this morning."

"Can he do that?" Velma asked.

"He can," Marnie confirmed, blowing out a long breath that seemed to communicate how defeated she was actually feeling. "When we signed the original lease, we weren't entirely happy with the location and hoped to find something better, so we only signed a six-month lease. When the six months were up, the landlord allowed us to go month to month. At the time, we were grateful for the flexibility a month-to-month lease afforded us. But as it turns out, the month-to-month agreement can be canceled by either party with a thirty-day notice. I thought we were protecting ourselves by signing it that way, but as it turns out, we were also protecting our landlord."

"Why does he want you out? Are you behind on your rent?" Velma asked.

"No." Marnie shook her head. "Nothing like that. The landlord found a new tenant who's willing to pay double the going rate if he can lease both our building and the building next door to the flower shop. The building next door has been vacant since the hardware store went out of business, so all our landlord needs is to get us out, and he'll be able to make a sweet deal."

"So what are you going to do?" I asked.

"We heard there might be an opening across the courtyard," Marnie said, a lilt of hope in her voice.

The bookstore was housed in its own building and enjoyed its own lawn and parking area, but there was a deli, a wine bar, a craft store, and an art gallery in a storefront one street over, and both the bookstore and the building with the wine bar shared a common courtyard that ran behind the buildings. The courtyard was a nice place to gather in the warmer months. The brick patio was artfully decorated with planter boxes featuring colorful flowers that provided a vivid contrast to the tranquility of the centralized fountain. There were several fire pit tables with chairs scattered about, making the courtyard a nice place to relax at the end of the day. Not that I'd taken advantage of the space at all since I'd been here, but I kept thinking that one of these days, I'd grab a book, buy a glass of wine, and put my feet up while the waterfall trickled in the background.

"I heard that the art gallery was thinking of moving," Velma said. "I don't know that a decision has been made, but if you're interested, you should talk to the landlord right away. If the space does open up, I have a feeling that it will go fast."

"I'm going to call him today," Marnie said. She looked at Velma. "I don't suppose you know the guy. You seem to know everyone in town."

"As it happens, I do know the landlord," Velma answered. "His name is Gaylord. He's not a bad guy, but he isn't going to make his choice based on whether or not he knows or likes an applicant. He's all about the money. What I'm trying to say is that if he's willing to lease the place to you, you're going to need to pay whatever amount he's asking for. He's not the sort to haggle, which I think is most likely why the art studio is thinking about moving."

"Do you think it's going to be expensive?" Cricket asked Velma.

"Since the building is basically bay-front property, there are a lot of vendors who would love to go in there, so yes, I do think the rent will be high. I remember two businesses had been in a bidding war for the space a while back. In a way, I'm surprised the craft store won out since it would seem that the liquor store that tried to lock down the location would have been better able to afford the high-end storefront."

"Perhaps Ethel made some sort of a deal with Gaylord," I suggested, referring to Ethel Covington, the owner of A Bit of This and That.

"I guess we'll need to look at our budget, but we are pretty desperate since we only have a month to be out of our current location, and being so close to y'all would be fun," Marnie said. "It'd take some finessing to get the budget to work out, but it would be awesome to be just across the courtyard from y'all."

"We could sit in the courtyard and have lunch together," Cricket added.

"I love the idea," I said. "I'm not sure that there's anything I can do to help you with the landlord but if you work it out, I'll help you move."

"That," Marnie smiled, "would be very helpful indeed."

Chapter 3

As promised, Alex came by with her golden retriever Cooper just after the bookstore had closed to the public for the lunch hour, and Hazel came back about ten minutes after that.

"Gwen's husband, Calvin, died while fishing off Sandbar Cove almost two months ago," Hazel informed us after Cricket asked about the man she'd heard of but had never met. "He was alone on this fishing trip, so no one knows exactly what happened, but it appears that he fell from the boat and was unable to get back onboard."

"Was he found in the water?" Marnie asked.

Hazel shook her head. "His body was found on the beach. It washed up a little over a mile east of Sandbar Cove several days after the man had gone missing. According to what I've heard around town, his boat was found about half a mile southwest of the last place Calvin was seen."

"So the boat drifted in one direction, and the body drifted in another?" Cricket asked.

"That's the way it appears," Hazel said. "I know it makes no sense that the boat would drift in one direction and the body would drift in the other, but Colt was able to track down two witnesses who saw Calvin fishing from his boat off Sandbar Cove on the day he was first reported missing, and while he wasn't sure where Calvin went after he left that spot, Colt did know he was there at one point."

"I guess it might seem odd that the body and the boat ended up in different locations, but currents can be tricky," I said. "The boat would be heavier and remain on the surface while the body could have been pulled under where it might have gotten caught up in a different current. Did Colt think the man died from drowning?"

"The official cause of death was never determined, but everyone suspected drowning," Alex informed us as she entered the conversation. "I pulled the police report before I came over since I figured that Calvin Harbinger's death might come up during a conversation relating to the death of his widow."

"So the real question is why was Calvin in the water in the first place," I stated.

Alex shrugged. "I wasn't here when the man's body was found, so I can't speak to the validity of any rumors that might have been going around at the time, but according to the police report, it appears as if the cause of death could never be determined due to the extensive damage to the remains. It was theorized that either the man had fallen overboard and was rendered unable to reboard, or he had been pushed by someone intending to do him harm."

"Extensive damage?" Cricket asked.

"Keep in mind that the remains were in the water for several days before the body washed up on the beach," Alex said. "During that time, the body traveled close to a mile. Likely even further than a mile if the location where the man entered the water was actually further out to sea than the location where he was last seen alive."

"So the remains would have been subjected to circumstances that would have left a lot of damage," I said.

"Damage such as tiny fish nibbling and predators snacking?" Cricket asked.

Alex nodded.

"Or broken bones caused by the remains being slammed up against the reef?" Marnie asked.

Alex nodded once again.

"So the coroner was never able to find obvious signs of foul play?" I asked.

"No. Not really," Alex answered. "Harbinger's skull suffered serious damage on the left side just above and behind the ear. There was also a large crack in the front above the eye sockets. The damage to the skull could have been caused by a head injury prior to his death, but it just as likely could have been caused by the reef."

"But it is possible that he might have been hit in the head prior to going overboard," I jumped back into the conversation.

"It is possible, but as I said, there's no proof of that," Alex reached down to pet Coop on the head. "Due to the fact that the man was seen alone on his boat earlier on the day he was first reported missing, the only conclusion that anyone was able to come to was that he fell. Having said that, Colt scribbled a bunch of question marks in the margin of the initial report he took at the scene. That caught my attention, so I called him. He told me, off the record since the case has been officially closed and further investigation wasn't warranted, that he never felt totally confident that this experienced seaman who'd been fishing his whole life just happened to fall overboard without provocation on what had been an extremely calm and almost waveless day. It was Colt's opinion that something more must have occurred, but he could never prove that, and, as I've already said, the witnesses all said that it appeared that Calvin was alone on the boat when he was last seen."

"Were any theorics seriously considered other than a theory that simply involves this man tripping and falling into the water?" Cricket asked.

Alex hesitated and then answered. "Yes, and no. As I mentioned, the coroner listed the official cause of death as unknown, but most felt he'd drowned.

Given the fact that the body washed up on the beach, drowning fits the narrative, although there was never any proof one way or another."

"So there wasn't any evidence of a stab wound or gunshot injury," I confirmed, figuring that either might have left a mark on a bone.

Alex nodded. "That's correct. While there was no specific damage to the remains that could be attributed to an act of violence, as I already said, the remains were so badly damaged that it's difficult to know what might have led to the man's death. I can say that Colt didn't find anything definitive inside the boat to support the theory of a violent end, such as blood spatter or other signs of a struggle. Without proof of foul play, the only conclusion that anyone looking into it could come to was that a terrible accident had occurred."

"Unless there was reason to suspect foul play," I said. "Was there ever any indication that a motive for murder might have existed? Or might there have been other details that just didn't fit?"

"Actually, a few things did stand out in Colt's mind as being suspect," Alex said. "Unfortunately, none of the little red flags he discovered ever amounted to anything."

"What sort of red flags?" Velma asked, jumping into the conversation for the first time.

Alex answered. "For one thing, Colt told me that Gwen had shared that it was extremely unusual for Calvin to head out fishing on a Sunday. He worked a lot of hours, many times from sunup to sundown, six days a week, but he always took Sunday off. Gwen was shocked when Calvin got up early that morning and told her he was going fishing. She asked him about it, and he just said that his catch that week had been on the light side, and the boat needed some repairs, so he felt he had some catching up to do."

"Wouldn't a commercial fisherman have taken a crew?" I asked.

"He would and did during the Monday through Saturday outings," Alex confirmed. "The crew wasn't asked to come in Sunday, and while Calvin's boat had been equipped for commercial fishing, according to everyone who remembered seeing the man that day, he was line fishing in fairly shallow water less than half a mile offshore, rather than net fishing."

"So it sounds as if Calvin lied to his wife about his real reason for going out that day," Marnie said.

"Perhaps. Colt believed that to be the case, although I'm not as sure," Alex said. "I do know that there was a rumor going around at the time the body was found that seemed to suggest that Calvin might have contributed to his own death."

"Suicide?" Velma asked. "Why?"

"I'm honestly not sure," Alex admitted. "As I said, I wasn't even in town when this all went down, so I can't speak to any rumors that might have been going around at the time, but it had been suggested that Calvin was stressed to the point of being despondent. Based on notes Colt left in the file, it seems that the man had suffered from a drinking problem in the past, which at one point prompted Colt to look for proof of alcohol consumption on the boat. He never found any. In fact, the only beverages he found onboard were a few colas and a half-empty pitcher of iced tea."

"Okay, so if he hadn't been drinking and hadn't committed suicide, what else might have been going on?" Cricket asked.

Alex responded. "Gwen mentioned to Colt that Calvin had been moody in the weeks before his death. She wanted him to go to the doctor since she felt that his mood swings were organic in nature and likely caused by a medical issue or chemical imbalance rather than stressors in his life. Colt wasn't sure he agreed with that assessment, but he did admit that it was a consideration."

"Gwen had been into this new health thing," Hazel said. "She changed her diet, started taking yoga classes, and even started drinking a new tea she imported from somewhere in South America. The tea supposedly was the key to a long life."

"That may explain the pitcher of tea Colt found on the boat, but I can't be sure at this point," Alex said.

"So, did Colt think that Calvin was having personal issues and simply needed time to get away, which was the real reason he went fishing on a Sunday?" Cricket asked.

Alex nodded. "Basically, yes. Colt found evidence of both financial issues as well as health issues. Colt's opinion was that Calvin simply needed time to process things."

"Do you know if Calvin ever went to the doctor?" Velma asked Alex.

"I'm not sure. There isn't mention of it in the file."

I glanced at Hazel, who didn't know whether or not Calvin had ever gone to the doctor as several people had suggested he should.

The idea that Calvin may have been ill seemed important. Might he have been seriously ill? Perhaps even terminal? If he was suffering from something life-altering or even life-ending, it would explain why Gwen was importing tea from South America despite their having financial issues, and it might give justification to the idea that the man went out for one last hurrah and then decided to take his fate into his own hands and end things. Of course, something like that would show up on the autopsy. Wouldn't it? Alex had said the remains were damaged, but in my mind, damaged wouldn't necessarily indicate not intact. I hated to ask Alex about it in front of Hazel, so instead, I asked about the crew. "I assume the crew members were interviewed."

Alex nodded. "Colt spoke to the men both individually and as a group. During the individual interviews, there was some discrepancy as to whether or not the team had caught their limit that week, but overall, it appeared that while the group was doing okay, they hadn't been reaching their goals."

"Did Calvin's men think it was likely that Calvin would set out on his own?" I asked.

Alex answered. "Colt told me that the general consensus was that Calvin would have called his men in if he was heading out to sea to do some serious fishing. If he just wanted to dip a rod in the water while he worked on whatever had been troubling him, then it did seem likely he would have gone alone."

"And the part about the boat needing repair?" Cricket asked. "Did that track?"

"I think those old fishing boats are always in need of repair," I said.

"So what are we saying here?" Velma asked. "Do we think the events that led up to Calvin's death are relevant to what happened to Gwen? I feel like this conversation started in one place but ended up in a totally different place."

"Even though we originally got together to discuss Gwen's death, in my mind, this seems relevant," Marnie said.

I agreed. "If Calvin was pushed from the boat, then someone likely did so with the intent to murder him. I'm not saying that's what happened, but knowing whether Calvin's death was an accident, the result of an act of violence, or even self-inflicted does seem to matter. The problem is that there doesn't seem to be a way to determine what went down that day with any degree of certainty. And even if we are able to make a statement relating to Calvin's death, we'd still need to decide if the same statement can be made in relation to Gwen's death."

"You're thinking that if Calvin was pushed, then it seems possible that the same person who killed

Calvin might have had a reason to kill his widow as well," Cricket stated.

I nodded.

Alex jumped back into the conversation. "I think it's possible that if Calvin didn't simply slip and fall off the boat and Gwen didn't kill herself, then it's likely that the two deaths are related. The problem, at this point, as we've said on more than one occasion, is that we really have nothing to prove anything. When I spoke to Colt, he didn't seem confident that I would be able to find anything to hang my hat on. Colt shared that when he investigated Calvin's death, he searched for alternative explanations to the slip and fall theory, but Colt never got anywhere. Without a witness who might have seen another passenger on Calvin's boat, or at least a witness who might have seen another vessel in the area, he really had nothing. As I mentioned, no blood was found on the boat, at least not human blood. Calvin did have a fishing boat, so a lot of fish blood had seeped into the decking and stained it.

"What about other sorts of physical evidence?" Hazel asked Alex.

"Lots of prints and fibers were processed and included in the report, which would be expected since a crew usually occupied the boat. A handful of people had seen Calvin alone on the water, and nothing indicating Calvin wasn't alone when he went into the water was identified."

I was about to ask a question relating to the identities of some of the crew members when Alex's cell phone dinged three times.

She removed the cell phone from her pocket and looked at the display. "I'm sorry, but the mother of my missing teen has arrived early for her interview. I'm going to need to go."

"Who's missing?" Velma asked.

"A high school student named Bradley Boxer. Do you know him?"

Everyone agreed that the name didn't sound familiar.

"I think his family only recently moved to Holiday Bay," Alex said, motioning for Coop to come with her. "I've enjoyed chatting with the five of you, but I really do need to go."

"Before you go, can you answer one question?" Hazel asked.

"Sure, if I can."

"Are you planning to investigate Gwen's death?"

Alex looked Hazel in the eye. "I am open to the idea that Gwen's death was not a suicide, but as I've already indicated, I really have nothing to go on other than a gut feeling that more is going on than would appear on the surface. I do plan to dig around, but at this point, that's all I can promise."

"That works for me," Hazel said.

The rest of us agreed.

After Alex left, Velma, Cricket, Marnie, Hazel, and I continued to explore different theories, none of which ended up getting us anywhere. Eventually, Hazel left, and Marnie and Cricket returned to their flower shop. "Do you really think that Gwen might have been murdered?" I asked Velma, who was busy building shelves along the back wall of the bookstore we planned to use as a coffee and pastry bar.

"I think it's a real possibility," she answered. "I hate to think that there is anyone in our little town who would kill a grieving widow, but the idea that Gwen simply gave up and gave into the darkness is a sobering one."

"I never had the pleasure of meeting Gwen, so I find that I'm unable to offer much of an opinion as to whether or not the woman would choose to end her pain, but Hazel seemed fairly adamant that there was no way Gwen would go there. You've been around a long time; what do you think?" I asked Velma.

Velma paused thoughtfully. She raised the screwdriver, pointing the standard head at the ceiling. "To be perfectly honest, I'm not sure. It is true that Gwen adores her three children, and I don't see her doing anything to hurt them. Her oldest son, David, lives in Albany. He's engaged to be married, has a good job, and seems pretty set. I imagine that losing both parents in such a short amount of time will be hard on him, but I don't anticipate that it will disrupt his life." She paused and took a breath. "Lily is a different story, however. Lily is the middle child and a junior in college. Lily's a nice girl, very polite and always ready with a smile. She seems to be doing well, but Lily's fairly immature for her age. I know that Gwen worried that the girl couldn't seem to manage her finances or take care of simple tasks such as renewing her driver's license or keeping her insurance policies current. She's also extremely unorganized and often finds herself in a bind due to that disorganization."

"And the youngest child?" I asked.

"Martin is just nineteen," Velma shared. "His father hoped he'd join his crew when he graduated high school, but Martin wasn't interested. He's drifted around a bit, borrowing money every couple of months until his father finally cut him off. I know he worked as a laborer for a while and then as a roadie for a band. I think Gwen mentioned a girlfriend, but I believe they broke up. I know Martin had talked a lot about traveling when he was a kid, but I seem to recall Gwen telling me that Martin was working for one of the airboat tour companies down in the Everglades."

"So it sounds as if the younger two may suffer from the lack of a parental figure in their lives," I said.

"That much is true," Velma agreed. "It's not that they aren't intelligent, and while I could be wrong, I imagine that if they were in a situation where there was no one to take care of them, they'd figure it out. Having said that, I know Gwen worried, probably more than she really should have."

Since I didn't have children, I found it hard to know with any degree of certainty what I would or wouldn't be willing to do for a child. Assuming that Gwen loved her children, as I imagined she had, it did seem unlikely that she'd willingly end her own life, leaving them to figure things out for themselves. Of course, not knowing the woman made it hard for me to guess what she may or may not have felt at the moment of her death. The pain of loss is an acute pain, which, if left unacknowledged and unattended, can burrow down into your soul until it is nearly impossible to find the person you'd once been.

Chapter 4

Most days, as long as I remained busy, I was able to deal with the curveball that life had thrown me in a productive manner. I'd managed to push through my grief and actually found happiness in the little things I once had. I tended to live in the now, so I suspected I might never again experience the exhilaration of making plans and striving to round that next corner in life, yet I felt that I'd found a steady place in my mind to live out my life, and most days, that was enough.

After tossing my keys on Vanessa's sofa table and setting Toby on the floor next to the overstuffed easy chair that filled one corner, I took a minute to acknowledge the silence. If I were honest, I'd have to admit that it was that first hour after arriving home at the end of the day that I still found the hardest. During this silence, I imagined Gus trudging home from work, shedding his work boots, and then asking what I had planned for dinner. He'd grab a beer, turn the TV on, and settle in with the local news. Sometimes, if Gus had something interesting to share, he would tell me about his day while I got dinner in the oven. I'd pretend to care about the moose his buddy, Linc, had bagged, and he'd pretend to care about the garden I wanted to put in that summer. We'd enjoy our meal and watch a favorite show or two before shuffling off to bed.

It was the routine I think I missed the most. The gentle knowing that at the end of the day, things would play out exactly as they always had, and for a brief moment, despite whatever else might be going on, life was predictable, and in that predictability, life seemed to make sense.

Slipping my shoes off, I shuffled into the kitchen, opened the cupboard, and took out a can of soup. After pouring the soup into a saucepan, I set it on the stove to heat while I looked for the cans of kitten food Hazel had left with me. Now that I knew for sure that Hazel was definitely not returning for the tiny baby who had been thrust into my care, I supposed I'd have to pick up some cat food and perhaps some toys. The idea of a cat bed briefly entered my mind, but after allowing Toby to sleep on the bed with me that first night, I knew a ritual that would likely last a lifetime had been established.

Once a bowl was filled with fresh water and Toby had been fed, I poured the soup into a bowl and carried it into the living room. I still liked to have the TV on while I ate, but watching the news brought back so many bittersweet memories that I usually opted for something Gus would never have watched, like a game show.

"Jeopardy is on tonight," I told the kitten. "The contestant they have this week is tough. He's been winning by a wide margin, so if you ask me, it's going to take someone exceptional to provide much of a challenge."

Toby curled up in my lap and started to purr. I set my mostly empty soup bowl on the coffee table in front of me as I melted into the serenity of his steady rumble.

"I've been thinking that we should get our own place," I said to the kitten as I gently stroked his silky head. "Vanessa has been nice enough to allow us to stay here while we figure out a long-term plan, but I know she wants to sell the house, and it really is too large for just the two of us."

The kitten rolled over onto his back, presenting me with his stomach to scratch.

"Are you listening to anything I'm saying?" I asked the sweet little furball. I smiled when he actually rolled back over, opened his eyes, and looked at me.

"A cottage near the water would be ideal, but I think it might be nice to be closer to the bookstore during the winter. The problem is there aren't a lot of houses in that area."

Toby jumped down from my lap and wandered into the kitchen. He'd gobbled up the food I'd given him before I'd eaten my soup, so perhaps I'd give him a little more. He'd been so skinny when I first got him that I figured an extra scoop of wet food here and there really wouldn't hurt.

"There's the space above the bookstore," I told the kitten as I opened another small can of food. "It's tiny, but it would be convenient to just head up the stairs at the end of the day. The space is currently being used for storage, so I'd need to figure that out. Additionally, the second floor is windowless, so I'd need to add some. It would be expensive, but having an unobstructed view of the bay from the second floor would be fabulous." I set the bowl with Toby's second serving of cat food on the floor. "I figure there's enough room for a small kitchen, single bedroom, small seating area, and functional bathroom. I'm used to bigger, but I think a scaled-down living area will suit me now that it's just the two of us."

I had to admit that I was warming up to the idea.

"I suppose it wouldn't hurt to have Lonnie come by and take a look. The space will only work if we can add windows, so I'll need to confirm that there isn't a structural reason that windows can't be added." Not only was Lonnie Parker my friend, but he was the contractor who was remodeling a portion of the bookstore into a coffee and pastry bar and a cozy reading lounge.

I headed back into the living room just as the double jeopardy round began. I sat on the sofa as the TV provided background noise, and I tried to picture my life in a tiny second-floor apartment. I'd put both the living area and the bedroom in the back of the space so that both rooms would have views of the bay. I'd put the kitchen and tiny bathroom in the front of the space, which, depending on where I put the windows, would look out over the sidewalk and possibly the parking lot. A window seat on the bayside would be lovely, and the wall between the two spaces could feature built-in bookcases to hold my books and the trinkets I chose to keep from my old life. The space would be so small that I wouldn't want to have walls that weren't absolutely necessary, so perhaps the kitchen and the living area could be divided by nothing more than a breakfast bar where I could eat my meals.

I opened my eyes and looked down at Toby as he slept in my lap. Maybe he was going to be a cuddler after all. He really was a cute little thing. I hadn't even known that I needed a pet in my life, but now that I had him, I realized he was exactly the companion I'd been waiting for.

When the end credits for Jeopardy started rolling on the screen, I considered just turning the TV off, but it was still early, and I didn't think I was ready to be alone with my thoughts. Grabbing the remote, I channel-surfed until I eventually settled on reruns of a show I'd seen on many occasions. Setting the kitten aside, I got up and headed for the kitchen. Perhaps a cup of chamomile tea would help me transition into a state of mind more conducive to sleep. I turned the kettle on and then glanced out the window at the drops of moisture that had dampened Vanessa's patio furniture. I hadn't realized we were supposed to get rain tonight. Not that it was really raining. But for the first time, I noticed heavy clouds had completely covered the moon, creating an inky darkness I found somewhat spooky. Most times, I liked the rain just fine, but there were occasions since Gus had been gone when the heavy dampness felt almost suffocating.

Once the kettle whistled, I poured the hot water over my premeasured tea leaves and left the tea to steep. I remembered that Gwen had begun using a special tea blend to make herself feel better. I wasn't usually the sort to want to partake of food or beverage items that were considered experimental in nature, but in this case, based on what others had said, it did seem as if the tea had led to an improved quality of life. Perhaps I'd look into it a bit deeper. A burst of energy would be welcome most days of the week.

Settling into one of Vanessa's oversized wingback chairs. I set my cup of tea on the table next to the chair, adjusted the light from the lamp, clicked on the gas fireplace to chase away the dampness, pulled a comforter over my lap, and picked up my book to read. I had never been a huge reader, but it did occur to me that if, in theory, I was going to lead the book club discussion each week, I really should, at the very least, read the chosen book. This week's book was a thriller that started out interesting but began to sag in the middle. In all fairness, it was likely that the book was just fine, and my inability to enjoy the simple pleasures in life was the real problem.

Toby jumped into my lap and began to purr. I closed the book, set it aside, closed my eyes, and drifted off into the land of possibilities, where loved ones didn't die and dreams for the future never came to an abrupt end.

Chapter 5

"When I called Lonnie to ask him about coming by to look at the storage space above the bookstore, he told me that he received a call from the guy at the granite company, letting him know that the granite we picked out for the countertops in the coffee bar has been placed on backorder," I said to Velma the following morning.

"I thought the granite was in stock when we ordered it," Velma said.

"Lonnie said that he was told the granite was in stock, but apparently, someone messed up and reserved the wrong thing. Lonnie said that we could wait for our original choice to arrive, but he stressed that it might be as long as another month or possibly two before it comes in, or we can cancel our order and pick out something else. The vendor we ordered the granite from originally has some other items in stock that we can look at, or Lonnie said we can head to Portland or even Bangor and see if there is something in stock at one of the larger dealers we can have shipped right away. When I asked him if it mattered to him, he said it didn't. He assured me that he will make the time to oversee the installation whenever it arrives."

Velma paused and looked in my direction. She leaned a hip against a recently installed cabinet as she seemed to be thinking things through. "On the one hand, I really love the granite we picked out and would hate to spend eternity with granite we like less simply because of a delay, but on the other hand, I really do want to get my coffee and pastry bar finished so we can open before the rush during leaf season. We should probably go ahead and go to Portland and check out the options. We might find something we like even better."

I nodded. "That was my thought as well. I'll call Lonnie back and have him make an appointment for us to speak to the sales staff at the warehouse. When do you want to go?"

"Sunday works best for me, but the granite warehouse is likely closed. Let's go ahead and close the bookstore tomorrow and do it then."

Closing the bookstore on a weekday wasn't ideal, but we'd been closed off and on during the remodel, and most local folks were used to our irregular hours by this point. We really did need to hire a part-time counter person to handle things when Velma and I were away, but we simply hadn't gotten around to hiring anyone quite yet.

"So why did you want Lonnie to come by to look at the space above the bookstore?" Velma asked, coming back around to my original comment.

I shared my idea to convert the space into a small apartment for Toby and me with her.

"I like that idea," she responded. "Not only will having living quarters right upstairs be convenient for you but once we begin taking on the rescue cats, there will be someone on the property twenty-four seven, so we won't need to worry about moving them at the end of each day."

"I hadn't even thought of that, but you make a good point; although, I do hope my social life improves a bit, and I'm not actually here twenty-four/seven."

Velma laughed. "Of course, I didn't mean twenty-four/seven literally. I just meant that there would be a regular presence if you lived on the property."

"I agree. And I'm really excited to finish the remodel, so I can settle in with Toby and we can find our new groove. Lonnie's coming by to look at the storage space tomorrow afternoon, so how about we go and look at the granite in the morning."

"That sounds good to me," Velma responded as I headed into the office to call Lonnie back and fill him in on our plan. He was going to call the granite warehouse to make our appointment. The last thing I wanted us to do was to make the trip to Portland, only to find they were closed.

"Hey, y'all," Cricket said in a singsong voice as she breezed in like a breath of fresh air on a hot summer day.

"Morning, Cricket," I said as the young florist spun around, which sent the skirt of her pretty yellow dress twirling around her. "Is Marnie with you?"

"She's parking the car," she informed me as she sidled up next to me, smelling of lilac and something fruity. Maybe peaches. "We have the best news."

"I like good news," I said. "Care to share?"

"I should wait for Marnie." She crossed her arms over her chest, showing off recently polished nails. "Let's just say we're going to be neighbors."

"You leased the space in the shop across the courtyard," Velma guessed.

"We did." Cricket began to bounce up and down.

"I thought you were going to wait for me before telling them," Marine complained after coming in from the sidewalk.

"I did wait, but they guessed."

"Congratulations to both of you," I said, opening my arms to Cricket, who came in for a hug. I'd never been much of a hugger before meeting the lively southern belle who seemed to consider every situation a huggable moment.

"I was expecting a real uphill battle," Marnie said. "But I made an appointment with the landlord and laid out my reasons for wanting to rent his space and my willingness to pay a reasonable rent. He seemed to like the idea that he would have a quick turnaround and wouldn't need to advertise for a renter or sort through applications as part of that process. I only chatted with him for about thirty minutes before he handed me a contract and a sheet with specific terms, and we were shaking hands on a move-in date in just three weeks."

"It's going to be tight to get everything moved from our current location before the lease on that place runs out, but we can do it," Cricket said. She clapped her hands together. "I really haven't been this excited since Alva May Bell was caught cheating on her math test just before the big homecoming game, and I was voted in as homecoming queen after she was disqualified."

I had a feeling there was a fun story there, but I decided not to ask.

"I'm so happy for both of you," Velma said. "I'm sure knowing that you have time to get settled somewhere new before your old lease expires has relieved a lot of the pressure you were feeling."

"Oh lordy, ain't that the truth of it all," Cricket said, looping her arms through Marnie's and dragging her toward the backdoor that led out into the courtyard.

Velma smiled at me as the sisters could be heard speaking at a volume that seemed to exceed what would be considered necessary. "I have a feeling that things around here are about to get a whole lot noisier," she said.

"I like noisy," I said. "Maybe not all the time, but after Gus passed away, I found I no longer appreciated the quiet."

"I can understand that. It's a different experience to want to be alone with your thoughts than it is to be alone because no one is there. I spent some uncomfortable alone time myself before Royce came back into my life."

Marnie and Cricket breezed back in from the courtyard and out the front door with nearly as much fanfare as they'd demonstrated when they'd breezed in. There was something about the sisters that simply screamed energy. I smiled as I thought back over moments in my own life when I'd been happy enough to wear that happiness on my sleeve for all to see. It'd been a while. Too long, I realized.

"I do enjoy those girls," Velma said, mirroring my thoughts, as she returned to the shelves she'd been installing, and I returned to my inventory.

I unpacked three boxes and stocked them on the proper shelves before I realized it had been a while since I'd seen Toby. He'd been sleeping in the large window seat earlier, soaking up the sunshine as it streamed in from the east. "Have you seen Toby?" I asked Velma.

"Not for a while, now that you say that." She stopped what she was doing. "I hope he didn't get out when the girls went to look at the courtyard."

We both headed toward the back door, which was closed now but had been left open while the sisters were outside. Stepping out into the courtyard, I looked around. I didn't see the little furball near the fountain or on one of the benches that lined the fire pit. He'd shown interest in the birdbath in the past, so I headed in that direction. A breeze was blowing in off the sea, which sent the chimes singing. Generally speaking, Toby wasn't fond of the high-pitched jingle. I was about to check the little grassy area near the deli when Velma announced that she'd found him.

"Where was he?' I asked as she stepped forward with the kitten in her arms.

"He was sleeping down in the flower bed near the poppies. I could barely see him with all the orange."

I took the kitten from Velma's outstretched arms. "If we are going to showcase cats from the local rescue, it's obvious that we need to do a better job with the door. Maybe a double-door system with multiple signs to remind folks to close the door behind them."

"I think a better idea might be to keep the cats in an area away from the exterior doors, as we've previously discussed. I still like the double-door scenario, which is similar to the double-gate system employed by the dog park. If the cat room doesn't open to the outside, we'll have extra protection if one of the felines manages to escape."

"In that scenario, if they escape from the cat room, they'll only end up in the main part of the bookstore rather than outside."

"Exactly."

It occurred to me that allowing the cats to be showcased at the bookstore was going to be a much bigger responsibility than I'd first imagined. Not that I wasn't willing, but Toby going missing even for a few minutes made me realize that an exceedingly reliable system to protect the cats would be absolutely necessary.

Chapter 6

Velma and I had just finished the ham and turkey sandwich, tub of potato salad, and potato chips we'd shared from Surfside Deli when Alex and Coop entered the bookstore through the back door, which opened out into the courtyard.

"I have news," she said with a smile as Coop came over to say hi to me and Alex hopped up onto the counter, crossed her legs under her body, and seemingly settled in for a lengthy explanation.

"News about Gwen?" I asked.

She picked up a pickle that had been sitting on a paper plate with a few leftover potato chips from our lunch and took a bite from the end. "Sort of. I still haven't found anything that would definitively indicate whether Gwen's death was due to suicide or murder, but I was able to convince one of Calvin's crew members to share what he knew about Calvin's overall demeanor during the weeks leading up to his drowning. The crew member confirmed a lot of what we've already figured out. Calvin seemed to be having a hard time financially. Not only wasn't he pulling in near the catch that he'd planned to, but the price of seafood, in general, had dropped, and he'd missed some days on the water due to illness. In addition to the dip in income, his boat was in desperate need of repair, and even though he'd been patching it together, the patch job wasn't going to last much longer.

"Maybe he could have gotten a loan," I suggested.

Alex responded. "According to my source, Calvin had taken out a loan the previous winter and used his fishing boat as collateral. He'd been unable to get back on track, so borrowing additional money against the boat most likely wouldn't have happened. In addition to being unable to pay his crew, he was in danger of losing his boat and livelihood." She took another bite of the pickle and continued. "The crew member I spoke to seemed to think the crew was on the verge of mutiny. Calvin owed them money, and while they'd tried to be patient with the guy, they had rent or mortgages to pay and, in some cases, families to feed. My source felt it was likely that even if Calvin hadn't died, he would have lost his boat and his crew before the end of the summer. My source admitted that he had feelers out since finding a good solid boat to hire on with isn't always all that easy, and realized that if he didn't want to be homeless over the winter, he better start making some serious cash this summer."

"So what are you saying?" Velma asked, joining in on the conversation.

"I'm not sure," Alex admitted. "My first thought was that it sounded as if Calvin Harbinger had as much of a motive to end his own life as his wife Gwen had, but the crew member I spoke to didn't think that was what had happened. He didn't think Calvin had simply slipped and fallen into the water and then drowned after he was unable to climb back up, either. Calvin was a good swimmer who'd worked on the water his entire life, so unless there'd been some huge storm with giant swells that might have knocked him overboard, he wasn't buying the slip-and-fall explanation. Although, after I mentioned the head injury, he did admit that hitting your head and passing out or even simply getting dizzy could cause even a good swimmer to drown. Still, even with the head injury, it was the crew member's opinion that Calvin was pushed."

"It's going to be hard to figure that whole thing out unless there was a witness," I said.

"Unfortunately, that's true," Alex admitted. "Calvin had been fishing off Sandbar Cove, but no one saw what happened, so no one knows with any degree of certainty that he entered the water in that area. It was the opinion of the man I spoke to that Calvin had pulled up anchor and moved on from that location by the time he went into the water. The water off Sandbar Cove is shallow and not the best spot for fishing, so he didn't know why he would have been there in the first place, but if his real intent was to sit a spell and have some time with his thoughts, then perhaps the quality of the fishing wasn't that important."

"Or he was there for another reason," I said.

"I thought of that," Alex said. "Even if Calvin was half a mile out, it would have been easy for someone with a surfboard to paddle out and meet up with him. The day he went missing was a calm day with few breakers. I'm not sure why you'd go about meeting up with someone in this fashion, but it would have been possible."

"So even though no one saw another boat in the area, it's possible that Calvin's boat was boarded," Velma confirmed.

Alex nodded.

"Any idea why anyone would do that?" I asked.

"Not really," Alex answered. "If Calvin and this potential visitor planned to meet up for some reason, it seems to me it would make more sense to simplify things and meet at a restaurant or at one of the bars in the area. Why go to all the trouble of having Calvin bring his boat to the cove and then have the person he was meeting up with paddle out? Where's the logic? But if the meeting hadn't been planned, and if Calvin really did anchor there simply to have some time to himself and fish, and if someone on the beach had noticed him and decided to paddle out, then Calvin may have been surprised by his visitor."

"Wouldn't Calvin have seen someone coming?" Velma asked.

Alex shrugged. "Perhaps. But he probably wouldn't have noticed if he was sitting with his back to the beach, or he'd fallen asleep, or perhaps had gone below for some reason. Or it's even possible he knew and welcomed his visitor, assuming, of course, that he even had one."

I supposed all of that was true. "Okay then," I asked, "if someone did paddle out and board Calvin's boat, why would that person shove him in the water?"

Alex finished the pickle she'd been nibbling on this entire time. "I'm not sure, but I suppose it's possible that Calvin and the individual, who we suspect may have boarded his boat, could have struggled, and Calvin might have accidentally gone overboard."

Velma stood up and headed toward the coffee counter, where she put a pot of coffee on to brew. "If Calvin had been knocked overboard accidentally, wouldn't you think the person who knocked him off the deck would have tried to rescue him?" Velma asked.

"That would seem to be the case if the whole thing had actually been an accident," I agreed.

"The man I spoke to mentioned more than once that Calvin owed people money," Alex circled back around. "And not just his crew. Unfortunately, he didn't seem to be able to come up with any names and just kept saying that the guy was in debt. Now, I don't know for certain that the man's death is related to his state of indebtedness, but it does seem that money turns out to be the motive for murder second only to love."

"Okay, so maybe Calvin owed money to the wrong person, and this person shoved him into the water and left him to drown," I said. "How on earth will you ever prove that?"

Alex jumped down off the counter and Coop came trotting over to stand next to her. "Right now, I'm following the money. If Calvin owed someone a lot of money, it seems as if there might be a trail to pick up. If there is a trail, I'll find it." She picked up an unopen bag of potato chips. "Are either of you going to eat these?"

"Help yourself," I said. "The deli has good sandwiches if you haven't had lunch yet."

"I don't have time to stop for lunch." She held up the bag. "These will tide me over. Thanks."

"Before you go, did you ever find that high school student you were looking for?" I asked.

"No," Alex answered. "But I have been able to verify that there are a few items missing from his room. My gut tells me he just took off. I'll continue to ask around, of course, but I really do think what we're dealing with is a runaway and not a victim of violence." She started toward the door, stopped, and turned around. "Say, it just occurred to me that if Calvin was in debt and his crew knew about it, then his wife likely knew about it as well. I don't suppose either of you heard anything about the trouble Calvin might have been experiencing from his wife before she died?"

"I didn't know Gwen," I said.

"And I've been away from Holiday Bay ever since I settled with the insurance company," Velma said. "I've only been back in town for a few weeks and hadn't run into Gwen before her passing."

"I guess you should talk to Hazel," I suggested.

"Perhaps I will." She held the chips up again, "And thanks again for the lunch."

"I like her," I said as she walked away with the sweetest dog I'd ever met. "You can tell she's smart, and she has moxie."

"I noticed that she seemed to do a good job of steering the conversation the way she needed to steer it," Velma said. "I really hope she sticks around. Colt needs a second in command he can really count on, especially now that his niece and nephew are living with him. A real partner and not someone who's just looking to do their time until they get a better offer."

"I've heard that he's had a lot of rookies."

Velma nodded. "Most lasted less than a year. The only staff who ever stuck around was Peach Sherwood. I think she left a huge hole when she was murdered."

"Gabby seems nice," I said.

Velma nodded. "She does seem nice. I think she'll do fine. Since I'd known Peach for so long, I imagine the problem in my eyes is that everyone they've tried in the position simply pales by comparison. I realize this woman deserves a chance to prove herself, and I fully intend to give her that chance. She has a certain spunk that I know Peach would approve of."

"I've heard nothing but nice things about Peach. What happened to her was a real tragedy. I'm really sorry I never had a chance to meet her."

Velma offered a sad smile. "I'm sorry as well. I think the two of you would have gotten along just fine."

Chapter 7

Velma and I decided to meet early and head into Portland, hoping to pick out new granite and still return to Holiday Bay in time to do a few things in the bookstore before it got too late. The bookstore had remained open during the remodel, but we'd been keeping irregular hours and dealing with dust and noise, so compared to what they should have been at this time of the year, sales were down significantly. Not that we were overly worried. We both had cash reserves that would see us through until the remodel was complete and things got back to normal, but we felt we owed it to our customers to even things out a bit. The current situation seemed to find us closing at random points in time.

"Did you leave Toby home alone?" Velma asked me.

"Actually, no. Nikki came by my house last night to introduce me to a young woman she thought would make an excellent employee for the bookstore, and when I mentioned that I was going out of town today, she offered to keep Toby until we got back. I guess she's off today and planned to head out to the inn and hang out with Haven. She thought the kitten would have a blast with the other animals." I referred to Nikki Peyton, a waitress at the Bistro, and Haven Hanson, the newest employee at the Inn at Holiday Bay.

"I'm sure he will," Velma agreed. "Haven's dog, Baxter, seems to enjoy cats, and I know Ramos and Molly will both adore the kitten."

I pulled onto the main highway and headed west. "The only one I'm concerned about is Rufus, who, as you know, can be cranky, but Nikki promised to keep an eye on Toby."

"Rufus can be cranky at times, but he's actually pretty gentle beneath the gruff exterior. So tell me about the potential employee Nikki brought by," Velma suggested.

I adjusted my visor and answered. "The girl's name is Eden Halliwell. She just moved to Holiday Bay a couple of weeks ago. She's twenty-four years old and seems really nice. When Nikki made a comment about Eden being a voracious reader, I asked about books she enjoyed, and it sounded like she enjoys novels from many different genres. Since neither you nor I are big readers, having someone around who's better able to make recommendations would be beneficial."

"I agree with that," Velma said. "How does Nikki know this girl?"

"I guess Eden went into the Bistro looking for work, but Shelby's in good shape after hiring your displaced employees. Nikki was there, and the two of them got to talking, and at some point along the way, Nikki realized that Eden would be a good fit for us. I wanted to discuss it with you before making a decision, one way or another, so I asked the girl to come back Monday. I figure we can both chat with her then."

"In terms of the hours she can work, does she seem flexible?" Velma asked.

"She said she was. I don't think she has a lot going on. I'm not entirely sure why she moved to Holiday Bay in the first place. After Nikki introduced the girl, we started talking about Toby and the cat lounge we're thinking about adding. Time seemed to slip away from me, and while I did ask for her references, I never had the opportunity to ask many questions about her background or work experience. If she shows up Monday, we can ask all our questions."

"Seems like Vanessa had several part-time employees when she ran the place," Velma pointed out.

"She did, but I know keeping employees was difficult for her. I'd rather have a full-time employee I can count on. We may not have full-time hours right now, but we will once we finish the remodel, so I figured I'd look for someone willing to grow with us."

"That sounds like a good plan. A good full-time employee will provide the flexibility for us to work the part-time schedule we discussed when we initially explored the possibility of forming a partnership."

As we neared Portland, the conversation segued to topics relating to the remodel. We weren't planning a large project, but we wanted the changes we did make to be well thought out and functional. The bookstore Vanessa had sold me had been an operating firehouse at one point, which meant it was steeped in history and already possessed a lot of charm. I didn't want to make changes that would detract from what was already there, so Velma and I discussed it with Lonnie, who helped us settle on minor changes that would allow us to add a coffee and pastry bar, a cozy reading lounge, and a separate cat lounge if that was the way we decided to go. The granite we were picking out today was for the coffee bar. It was just one counter, so we wouldn't need a large piece, but we hoped to find something that complimented the colors that already existed in the structure.

The granite warehouse Lonnie sent us to in Portland was huge, so it took us quite a while to look around, but we eventually settled on a dark gray slab with threads of light gray and black running throughout. The granite had a unique pattern that stood out amongst the rows and rows of samples. There was one black slab that I was drawn to, but with the bookstore's dark red brick on the walls, Velma and I decided that something with a lighter tone might work better. When it came time to pick out granite for my upstairs apartment, assuming I got that far and my vision actually became a reality, I wanted to find a deep blue. One of the suites at the Inn at Holiday Bay featured a bright blue granite with veins of a darker blue blending with a lighter shade. The granite reminded me of the changing moods of the sea, and when I first saw it, I knew that if I ever had my own space, I'd want something very similar.

After Velma and I took care of the paperwork and arranged for delivery of the granite per Lonnie's instructions, we headed back toward Holiday Bay.

"We never did have lunch," I said as we merged onto the highway that hugged the coast. "Should we stop somewhere?"

"There's a fun little seafood shack right on the water if you don't mind picnic benches and paper plates," Velma informed me.

"That sounds fine to me. Sometimes those little shacks have the best food."

"If you like seafood, you won't be disappointed. The lobster rolls are some of the best anywhere, and they have a seafood jambalaya that is to die for."

"Jambalaya? Really? Here in Maine?"

Velma nodded. "I know it doesn't sound like the sort of thing you'd get here, but the guy who runs the place was originally from Louisiana, so he has a few things on the menu that you'd be more likely to find in the south. The jambalaya is really unique. There's plenty of lobster, shrimp, clams, scallops, plus

Andouille sausage, peppers, spices, and rice. It's a bit on the hot side, but really very good."

"It sounds delicious. I think I'm going to try it."

"You won't be sorry you did."

Velma wasn't wrong about the food. It was delicious. And it was fun sitting side by side at a rickety picnic table with chipping paint as we watched the waves gently roll onto the rocky shoreline. I'd enjoyed my life in Minnesota, and in many ways, living in Maine was a huge adjustment that I was still coming to terms with, but I had my own business and friends that meant the world to me. More importantly, I had a new start, well away from the painful memories I'd left behind.

"Royce wants to know if you want to come out to our place for a cookout on the patio tonight," Velma said as she studied the text message on her cell phone while we drove east.

"This isn't a hookup, is it?"

Velma laughed. "No, we wouldn't do that. If we decide we have someone we feel you simply must meet, we'll tell you so upfront. Did your friends in Minnesota try to fix you up?"

I nodded. "All the time. Not at first, mind you, but once my tenure as a widow passed the six-month point, it seemed as if friends I hadn't seen for years were coming out of the woodwork to introduce me to their boss, cousin, or brother."

"Let me see who's coming," Velma said, texting Royce back.

I thought how considerate it was that Royce had taken the initiative to invite friends over and make the food arrangements while Velma was busy at the bookstore. It seemed my new friend had managed to snare quite the catch.

"Joel is coming and will be bringing Emma," Velma began. "You know Joel and Emma. George Baxter, who, as you know, is living out at the inn this summer, will be there, and he's bringing a guest named Savannah."

"I know Savannah. I've only spoken to her twice, but she's a very nice woman. Well-read and intelligent. Fun to chat with. Anyone else?" I asked.

"Royce invited Beck Cage, who may or may not stop by. He's been involved with a case, which, according to Royce, seems to be wrapping up, so if he can get away, he promised to stop by. He also invited Hazel, who seems to be struggling since the loss of her friend, but he couldn't get a good read on whether or not she'd come by."

"Is that it?" I asked.

"As far as I know. Even if someone else does show up, the sheer number of individuals invited deters from the dating vibe."

I turned off the main highway and onto the road heading into town. "I know you're right, of course, and an evening with good friends sounds perfect. I guess I'm still a bit gun shy after my experience with friends from my past, but I don't imagine anyone here in Holiday Bay cares about me enough to meddle."

"I care about you," Velma said. "But I won't meddle. I promise."

"That's good enough for me," I said as Velma responded to Royce's text, and I headed toward the parking area behind the bookstore. "And I'd like to come. Lonnie is coming by later this afternoon to discuss my idea about the apartment, but I can come by after that."

Chapter 8

Velma headed home to help her groom with the last-minute preparations for the dinner party while I stayed to wait for Lonnie. There always seemed to be shelving to do, so I decided to tackle that while I waited for my contractor to arrive. I'd just finished shelving the romances and was about to start on the mysteries when Wanda Anderson entered through the door leading out to the parking lot.

"Oh good, you're still here," she said, breezing in. "I wanted to pick up those special order books your message said had arrived."

"I have them right here under the counter," I said, setting a stack of books on the wooden surface next to the cash register. "The total is on the receipt I slipped under the cover of the top book."

Wanda set her pretty yellow purse on the counter and pulled her checkbook and a lovely pen with a logo for the new gym in town from her purse.

"Are you a member of the new gym?" I asked as I waited for the check.

She tried filling in the dollar amount on the check, but when the pen didn't work, she grabbed a piece of scratch paper and scribbled on it. When the pen still wouldn't write on the check, she tossed it aside and pulled another pen from her purse.

"No. I'm not a gym member, but my husband, Desi, is." She pursed her lips as she scrawled Firehouse Books on the check using an interesting-looking logo pen from a bookstore down the coast. She filled in the dollar amount and paused. "Desi is a changed man since he joined that gym. He's switched to a plant-based diet, stopped drinking, started taking supplements, and lost fifty pounds."

"I guess that's a good thing." It sounded like a good thing to me, but based on the tone of Wanda's voice, I wasn't sure she agreed.

She frowned as she ripped the check out of the checkbook and handed it to me. "You'd think all of that would be a good thing, but in our case, I'm pretty sure that the changes are going to be the end of our marriage."

I raised a brow. "Oh? How so?"

She rested an arm on the counter. "For one thing, Desi is no longer interested in doing all the things we used to enjoy doing as a couple. We used to have pizza and movie night at home every Friday. It was our thing. In fact, it was over pizza and a movie that Desi and I first fell in love. Every Friday night since that first 'friend date' when our eyes met over a can of Miller Lite, and we realized how well suited we were, we've ordered an extra-large meat lovers pizza from Mario's Pizzeria, bought a six-pack of beer, popped a bowl of buttered popcorn, and put on an action flick. Until Desi started going to that new gym, it was something we both looked forward to. Since Desi started his gym membership, all he wants to do on Friday night is hit the weight room for an intense workout, followed by some time in the steam room."

I supposed I could see how that would be a problem. "Have you thought about joining the gym as well?"

She shook her head. "It's not my thing. I loved our old life. Prior to joining the gym, Desi might not have had the six-pack abs he has now, but we were happy, and 'we fit.' We'd eat burgers and pizza, drink beer, and spend the weekends in front of the TV." She slid her pen and checkbook back into her purse. "Last weekend, he went on a hundred-mile bike ride. I can't even ride a bike unless it's one of those stationary exercise bikes, and then I'm only good for a mile or two." She blew out a long breath. "Desi is a totally different person now." She placed her pile of books in her canvas book bag. "I may be losing my husband, but at least I still have my stories."

I felt sad for the woman as she walked away with her Lighthouse Books book bag, but I couldn't fault her husband for wanting to get in shape and improve his health. Excess weight and the health issues that came with it had never been an issue for me, but I suspected that if it had been an issue, and I'd finally made a commitment to get healthy, I'd want my spouse to take the journey to health with me. Of course, I also understood why Wanda might feel resentment toward the new gym. Before it opened, her life had been comfortable. Now it seemed she might be faced with losing her husband or making lifestyle changes she didn't seem prepared to make.

Lonnie arrived right at five o'clock as he indicated he would. I showed him the space on the second floor and explained what I wanted to do. He didn't see any immediate problems with the idea, but he did want to have an engineer come in to look at the structural integrity of the building before adding the windows, and he said he'd need to take a closer look at the current plumbing and electrical before he could work up a bid. I assured him that all of that was fine, and he indicated that he'd make some calls Monday and then get back to me with a timeline and estimate.

After Lonnie left to go home to his wife and six children, I settled Toby with his dinner, a bowl of fresh water, and his cat box and then promised him I wouldn't be gone long. Having a cat whose needs I was going to have to take into consideration from this point forward might seem to be a burden to some, but somehow, it felt just right to me.

Velma knew I'd be arriving late, and she'd told me to just come around to the back when I arrived. I parked four doors down, and, based on the number of cars parked along the street, I was willing to bet that

Royce had invited a few more folks than Velma had mentioned. Velma and Royce both seemed to enjoy entertaining, and they had a lot of friends, so I supposed I shouldn't be surprised by the sheer number of bodies they'd managed to pack into their backyard.

"I'm sorry about the chaos," Velma said as she greeted me with a hug. "When I spoke to Royce earlier, he really did say he was inviting a few friends over. I had no idea this was his idea of a few friends."

"It's fine," I assured her. "I wanted to stop by and say hi, but I can't stay long. Toby is waiting for me at home."

Prior to Gus's death, I would have been the first to arrive at and the last to leave a gathering like this, but now I found too many people, particularly too many new people, to be just a bit overwhelming.

"I know this is a lot all at once, but Joel, Emma, George, and Savannah are sitting near the fountain. How about we go and say hi to them," Velma suggested.

I smiled and nodded. Velma had turned out to be a wonderful friend, and I appreciated the fact that she understood how I was feeling.

Once Velma had dropped me off with folks with whom I felt a certain degree of comfort, I actually began to relax and have a good time. It seemed odd that I'd even reacted the way I had. Anyone who knew me would call me an extrovert, and most times, I was the sort who liked to be right in the middle of things, but Gus seemed to have taken a part of me with him when he passed away. The part of me who had energy and joy for life. The part of me who was outgoing and curious and who relished the opportunity to meet new people. In the beginning, I'd assumed my personality change was simply part of the grieving process, but I was less sure about that now. The woman I was when I was married to Gus was very different from the woman who sat here now. Not better or worse, just different.

"How long will you be in town?" I asked Savannah. I'd first met her a few months ago when I'd come to Holiday Bay to watch the bookstore for Vanessa, and Savannah had been a guest at the inn. She'd gone home after her scheduled stay but had shared with me how much she enjoyed the friends she'd met here and how eager she was to return. Apparently, she'd returned even sooner than I'd predicted.

"I'm here for four weeks this stay, but Joel has convinced me to consider a move to the area. I'm not sure I want to do that quite yet, but I do enjoy the town and the folks who live here, and since retiring from teaching, I'm not sure I have a reason to stay where I am."

"Well, I, for one, agree with Joel. It would be nice to have you as a neighbor."

"Emma told me about the book club you run on Tuesday evenings."

I glanced at Emma and smiled. "To be perfectly honest, the Tuesday night book club has melded into more of a support group for women who like to gossip and get twisted up in the lives of those we share our space with, but I think you'd fit in just fine. There are some weeks when we never even open the book we all agreed to read, but in the end, I think that everyone comes away satisfied."

She grinned. "I like a good gossip session. Any news about the deceased woman who'd been a member of your group?"

I imagined that Emma had filled her in, but I decided to go ahead and start at the beginning. I shared a brief background about the series of events that led to her becoming a widow. By the time I'd gotten through this part, George, Joel, and Emma had joined the conversation. Once everyone was up to speed on Calvin's death, I shared what I knew about Gwen's demise. The question relating to whether her death was murder or suicide was a complicated one that wouldn't be solved here tonight, but the discussion that followed served to engage those I chatted with. We'd been chatting for about twenty minutes when Velma wandered over with Beck Cage. I didn't know Beck well, although I had met him. I knew he was a retired cop turned PI who was likely in his mid-sixties. He had a booth at the Bistro, commonly referred to as "Beck's Booth," that he used as an office, and he seemed to know most of the locals after only a few years in Holiday Bay as a resident.

"I hear we're talking murder over here," Beck said once Velma had made the introductions.

"We aren't actually sure if we are dealing with a murder or suicide, but the loss of a member of our community is the topic of discussion. Did you know Gwen Harbinger?" I asked.

"No," Beck replied. "But I did know her husband, Calvin. He had a fishing boat that he docked at the marina near the Bistro, and he and his crew would come in for drinks a few times a week. I was sorry to hear that he died."

"I don't suppose you've been able to form an opinion as to what might have happened to the man," George wondered.

Beck shook his head. "I've been out of town for the past month, so most everything I know about the incident is what I've managed to pick up from the staff and customers I speak to at the Bistro. When Calvin's body was first discovered, there didn't seem to be much debate as to whether he'd fallen overboard or if something else was going on, but it seems that other theories have popped up while I was away."

"I hadn't heard that there were theories other than accidental until after Gwen was found dead, so I don't think you are too far behind the narrative," I said.

"Hazel seems to know more about it than anyone I've talked to," Velma said. "I haven't seen her yet, but she mentioned that she might stop by this evening. I'll bring her over when she gets here. I'm not sure whether she'll have anything new to add to the conversation, but she knew Gwen better than most, and she seems to have insight into how Gwen would or wouldn't have responded to the challenges that had been thrust upon her."

Once everyone in the group who had information concerning either Calvin's or Gwen's death shared what they knew with everyone else, the topic of conversation segued toward matters relating to the sweetness of life during a Holiday Bay summer. Joel, George, Savannah, and Emma had been to the Bands on the Beach event and had enjoyed listening to bands from generations past as the sun set beyond the horizon. Velma and Royce had attended a wine and dinner pairing that sounded fabulous, and Beck shared his sailing plans for the following day and invited any of us who wanted to go to tag along with him. I was tempted since I loved to sail and hadn't been in a long time, but I had a lot to do to get settled into my new life and really wanted to work on the never-ending chore of unpacking all the boxes Vanessa had been storing and sorting their contents.

The sun had set, and the majority of the food had been consumed by the time Hazel arrived. I'd been on the verge of making excuses and heading home to Toby, but I could see that Hazel had something on her mind.

"Lily showed up today," she said. She looked toward Savannah, who I wasn't sure she'd ever met. "Lily is Gwen's daughter."

"How did that go?" Velma asked.

Hazel answered. "As can be expected, she's both overwhelmed and devastated."

"There is a lot to take care of when a loved one dies," Emma said.

Hazel nodded. "There is. To be honest, I don't think Lily is prepared to deal with any of it. I asked her about her brothers, and she said that David plans to come but won't be able to get away for a few weeks, and Martin seems to be MIA."

"MIA?" Beck asked.

"Gwen's youngest son has been working for a tour company in the Everglades, and Lily said she hadn't talked to him in a while. She tried calling him, but Martin wasn't answering his cell phone or returning any of the messages she left. She finally tracked down the tour company where he worked when she'd last spoken to him, only to find out he'd been fired almost a month ago. At this point, she has no idea where he is."

"The poor thing must be worried sick," George said.

"About her brother, no," Hazel said. "Martin is a flake who has disappeared in the past, only to show up on someone's doorstep when he needs money. Lily seemed to think he was fine, but she is worried about being saddled with all the work of settling their parents' estate on her own if David isn't able to rearrange his schedule. She didn't have any idea where to start. The poor thing wasn't even sure if she should have her mom cremated or buried in the cemetery."

"Was her father cremated?" I asked.

"He was," Hazel answered. "But Lily wasn't sure that was what he wanted."

"I feel so bad for the child," Velma said, even though Lily was an adult and not a child. "I'll reach out to her tomorrow. She worked as a waitress at the diner one summer while she was in high school, so the two of us are close. Well, at least closer than others who might reach out to her."

"Did she seem to have an opinion about what might have happened to her mother?" Savannah asked.

Hazel answered. "Actually, she did. Lily shared that she'd spoken to her mother just a few hours before I found her body and that she seemed fine. Her mother had mentioned she was attending a book club meeting that evening and seemed upbeat about it. Lily said that when she mentioned coming home for a nice long visit before the fall semester started, Gwen was excited about that. Lily seemed to think there was no way her mother took her own life."

"If Gwen didn't take her own life, then what happened?" Emma asked.

Hazel shrugged. "No idea."

"The setup seems odd for a murder," Beck said. "For someone to have killed Gwen via carbon monoxide poisoning delivered through engine exhaust, they would have had to have found a way to incapacitate her. Otherwise, Gwen would have simply gotten out of the car once she realized she was in trouble."

"I suppose she might have been unconscious," Joel said. "Of course, in order to render her unconscious, she would have had to have been slipped sedatives or knocked out due to a blow to the head. Does anyone know if a toxicology screen was part of the autopsy?"

No one knew, but Velma volunteered to call Alex and ask her if she'd received the autopsy report.

"What if she was already dead, and someone staged the scene to make it look like Gwen committed suicide," George wondered.

"That seems possible," I said. "Again, I suppose that would show up during an autopsy. It's only been a few days since Gwen passed away, but I think an autopsy would have been performed by now. Maybe before we get off on too much of a tangent trying to figure out possible methods of murder, we should find out what the official cause of death actually is."

Velma went ahead and called Alex, but she didn't pick up. This wasn't an emergency, so while Velma left a message, she didn't want to call the emergency number. It was getting late, and if Alex had an early day the following day, it was possible that she'd already turned in for the evening. After leaving a message, Velma commented that until recently, Colt had generally had two assistants at any one time. In my opinion, the police chief should have a minimum of two full-time assistants for a town this size.

I'd actually enjoyed the evening more than I thought I would, but I was tired and didn't want to leave Toby for too long. After saying my goodbyes to everyone, I thanked Royce for the delicious meal and then headed to my car. I planned to open the bookstore the following day but told Velma there was no reason for her to come in if she had plans. The coffee bar hadn't officially opened, and with all the construction that was going on, we weren't getting a lot of foot traffic either. Velma assured me she'd be in for at least part of the day unless Royce had made plans for them. She figured she would have spoken to Alex by then and that I'd want to hear about the conversation.

I thought about Gwen as I got ready for bed. Given Lily's conversation with her mother, I could understand why Lily felt so sure that her mother hadn't committed suicide. But I'd had a friend in the past who'd decided to end her own life, and like the conversation that Gwen had shared with Lily, the last conversation my friend had shared with her sister had reportedly seemed equally normal. Like Gwen, my friend had been upbeat and optimistic as she shared plans for the upcoming day with her sister, and like Gwen, my friend had ended her own life just a few hours after engaging in this seemingly normal conversation. I knew of other cases where there was more of a warning that things weren't quite right, but I suspected that in death, as in life, the way one might choose to handle things could vary dramatically.

Chapter 9

I got up early the following morning, allowing me time to enjoy a pot of coffee with Toby before I showered and prepared to head to the bookstore. Not that Toby had enjoyed any of the coffee, but he seemed pretty jazzed about the scrambled egg I gave him with his cat food. My mind had been overflowing with ideas since speaking with Lonnie the previous afternoon. I had a small space to work with, but not as small as I'd first imagined. There was an attic space above the second floor of the building, which had housed bunk beds for the firefighters on duty at one time, but was used for storage now. Lonnie had presented the idea of using the attic space as a sleeping loft, giving me more room on the main floor of my second-floor apartment. I found that I liked the idea quite a bit, but only if it worked out to put in all the windows I had planned. Without the windows, the project would likely die. Without the windows that would supply light and fresh air, the space on the second floor would be dark and stuffy.

"I wonder if there will be room in the attic space to include a small closet bathroom," I said aloud, even though Toby was the only one around to hear me. "I'm afraid I'm at the age where a trip or two to the bathroom is a necessity most nights, and I don't relish the idea of climbing down and then back up the stairs each time."

"Meow."

"Yes, I'm aware that twenty-year-old me wouldn't have given a sleeping space without a bathroom a second thought, but things change." I stood up and took my mug to the sink. "I guess we should get going if we're going to open the bookstore on time. Finish your breakfast. We'll be leaving as soon as I get ready."

I wasn't necessarily the sort to believe that Toby could understand what I was saying to him, yet it comforted me to talk to him all the same. I supposed having someone to talk to was one of the things I missed most about having someone to live with. Gus and I hadn't always gotten along. The fact that we loved each other was a given, but we both had strong personalities that tended to clash. Looking back, most of our epic battles were really over nothing important. Sometimes I wished I could go back and do things differently, but then again, there were times when I actually thought Gus and I worked because of our battles and not despite them.

After I'd showered, dried my long white hair, twisted it into a braid that fell down my back, and applied a light coat of makeup, I slipped into white capris, a sunny yellow top, and white leather sandals. When I'd lived in Minnesota, I'd worn khakis or blue jeans almost exclusively, but now that I owned a pretty little bookstore in a pretty little town, I felt the need to make a bit more effort with my appearance.

Once I was ready, I grabbed Toby, slipped him into his travel carrier, and headed into town. It was a lovely day on the bay, and I was sure there would be multitudes of locals and visitors alike wandering the streets, all looking for the perfect deal to round out their gorgeous Saturday. When I arrived, I found the bookstore locked up tight, which didn't surprise me since I really hadn't been expecting Velma to be in early or even at all. I knew that Velma wanted to work more of a part-time schedule and to be perfectly honest, I preferred flexibility in my schedule as well. I planned to hire at least one full-time employee and one part-time helper to fill in, but as long as the budget would tolerate it, I might consider extra help beyond that during the busy summer and holiday seasons. I hoped Eden worked out. She seemed like a nice girl, and when I explained about the construction and the unreliable hours we'd be open until the remodel was completed, Eden seemed okay with that. I'd checked her references, and everything seemed fine. As long as she returned Monday as she assured me she would, I planned to offer her the job on a trial basis.

After letting Toby out of his cat carrier, I turned the closed sign to open and then went around the bookstore and opened the blinds. The view of the bay was particularly gorgeous today. It was always an exceptional view, but there were currently wildflowers blooming on the bluff, which provided a splash of color that only lasted a few weeks every year.

I supposed I could make a pot of coffee, but just grabbing a latte and bagel from the deli seemed to be the most expedient way to accomplish what I needed to accomplish. I didn't want to leave the bookstore unattended for long, so I called over to the deli and placed my order with Andy, who, along with his brother, Eli, owned the place. In the morning, Surfside Deli sold bagels and coffee, and then from eleven o'clock until close, they sold sandwiches. I supposed that the fact that we were putting in a coffee bar would provide a bit of competition for the brothers in the morning, but Velma and I had each spoken to Eli and Andy, and they'd seemed fine with our new venture.

I'd learned through the gossip grapevine that the brothers had moved to Holiday Bay from Washington State three years ago. I wasn't quite sure what had prompted the move from one coast to the other, but they seemed to fit in really well, and so far, everyone I'd spoken to had mentioned that they enjoyed stopping to chat with the brothers almost as much as they enjoyed the mile high sandwiches they made.

"Morning, Andy, Eli," I greeted the pair as I grabbed my order from the counter. I slipped them a twenty, and they handed me my change. "Beautiful day."

"It is at that." Andy glanced behind me. "Are you going to be open today?"

"For a while. I have some inventory to get through and paperwork to tackle, so I figured I'd be open while I was handling that, but I'm not sure if Velma will be in or not, so I may close early." After slipping a five-dollar bill into the tip jar, I shoved my change into my pocket. "Toby is next door alone, so I should get going. I locked the front door and put a sign in the window, letting folks know I'd be back in five minutes, but you never know what the little guy will get into."

"I understand," Eli said, smiling down at his little dog, Rusty, who loved hanging out in the courtyard while his "daddy" was at work.

After I returned to the bookstore, I took the sign out of the window and unlocked the door. I supposed it might not be the best idea to try to be open today since I was here alone and I really did have a lot to do, but I hated to be closed on a Saturday morning, so I decided I'd play it by ear and see how it went.

Of course, as in life, it seemed almost a given that any plans I might make for the day would end up being altered.

"You here, Lou?" I could hear Cricket's sweet voice call out as I gathered the last few boxes of inventory I wanted to shelve today from the storeroom.

"In the backroom," I called back.

I could hear the clickety-clack of her heels as she hurried down the hallway.

"It's already looking better in here," she said as I shoved a box of bookmarks to the side and picked up a box full of recently delivered paperbacks.

"Velma and I have been working on clearing out the space. We have big plans for this place, which don't include an excessive storage area. Of course, we'll need some storage, but not the massive area Vanessa needed since she tended to stick things in this room and then forget about them. Seems like a waste of space to me."

"I agree in theory, although I will admit to having slight hoarder tendencies myself. Marnie is the sort who hates clutter, so she's always on me to keep the storage areas tidy, but I will admit that if not for her, I'd probably have a huge mess, even worse than what Vanessa left for you. Speaking of Vanessa, have you heard from her?"

"I spoke to her last week. She seems happy. Making a move such as the one she decided to make seems rash, and I will admit that I worried in the beginning, but she really does seem to have found a man she adores and a new life she's excited about."

"I guess that's important. Having a life that you can feel excited about."

I nodded. "It is. A life that has meaning and fulfills you is a gift not everyone is able to enjoy. I feel that I've been lucky. I had a wonderful life in Minnesota with Gus. After he died, I honestly felt as if I'd never be happy again, but now that I have my new life here in Maine, I have to say that I am happy. Really happy."

Cricket smiled. "I'm so glad to hear that. I wasn't going to mention it since I know you've been dealing with a lot, but during the past few weeks, it almost felt that the feisty woman who came to Holiday Bay to cover for her niece had been replaced with someone who was struggling."

I grabbed the box, turned the light off, and headed toward the front. "I suppose I haven't really stopped to consider how much making my move to Holiday Bay a permanent one would affect me. I loved Gus and will miss him every day of my life, but I honestly thought that after a year of intense grieving, I was through the worst of it. It seems that making my move from Minnesota a permanent one has reactivated some of those deeply buried feelings of sorrow." I set the box on the counter and looked directly at Cricket. "I hadn't even realized it, but I think that leaving Minnesota and the life I shared with Gus was a bit like leaving Gus. I suppose I needed to mourn his absence from my life all over again."

"I guess I can understand that. And I didn't bring it up to make you feel worse. I guess I've just been worried about you."

I reached out and hugged my young friend. "Thank you. I appreciate that. And I think I needed someone to remind me that no good can come from wallowing in the past. My memories mean so much to me, but I don't want to allow myself to become bogged down in immense pain again. I want to be able to remember Gus and my life with him with joy, not sorrow. To be honest, I wasn't even aware that I was slipping back into old patterns. Now that you brought it up, I guess I can see how my break from my old life was one I needed to spend time processing." I narrowed my gaze. "So, did you stop by to check in on me, or are you here for another reason?"

"Actually, I came by to take some measurements. Marnie doesn't think I should bother the folks over at the art gallery since they're busy preparing to move, but we need to make plans, and the space we're moving into is different in size and shape than the space we are moving out of."

"I agree that you need a plan, and I'm sure as long as you're quick, the art gallery folks won't mind if you stop by. I stopped by to chat with Astoria yesterday, and she told me that the art gallery will be out by the end of next week."

Astoria Walton was the owner of the wine bar the bookstore shared a common courtyard with along with the deli, craft store, and soon, the flower shop.

After Cricket scampered out toward the courtyard, which would provide a shortcut between the bookstore parking lot and the art studio, I returned my attention to my inventory. Of course, Cricket wandered back in after only fifteen minutes of dedicated book shelving.

"Did you get your measurements handled?" I asked.

"Sort of. I managed to get a few of the measurements I need, but the place is pretty torn up as they prepare to move, so it was hard to move around in there. I need to learn to be patient. It's such a nice day, and I need to decompress a bit, so I think I'll grab a cup of coffee and a bagel before heading back to All About Bluebells."

"It is calming to sit out by the fountain." I looked toward the front door. "I'll just lock up and join you. Trying to be open when there are so many distractions in addition to having so much on my mind isn't working anyway."

"If you hire Eden, you can do what you need to do, and she can handle the customers."

"Do you know Eden?" I asked.

She nodded. "Nikki brought her by the flower shop and introduced her to us. Nikki has apparently taken her under her wing and is helping her find a job."

"I liked the girl right from the beginning, but I wanted to check her references which I have now done. I would like for Velma to have an opportunity to meet her first, but I plan to offer Eden a full-time position if she's still interested. She didn't have a phone number to leave with me when she was here, but she promised to return Monday. I hope she does."

"Eden's cell phone, along with her purse, was stolen, but she said she planned to replace her cell phone today. I know that Eden has been staying with Shelby while she's looking for a job."

"Really?" I raised a brow.

"Shelby has a full staff right now and didn't have any shifts to offer her, but she felt bad for the girl, so she offered her a place to stay until she's able to get settled."

That's one of the many reasons why I loved this town. There were so many genuinely good people who seemed to really care about their neighbors.

I followed Cricket out to the courtyard and sat near the fountain. Once I'd settled Toby on the ground with a long leash so he could walk around without wandering off, I took my cell phone out of my pocket. "I'm going to call Shelby and let her know that I plan to offer Eden the job. Maybe she can pass the message along. If Eden isn't busy, perhaps she can come by today to complete the new hire paperwork. I figure I'll be at the bookstore for at least another couple of hours."

"That's a good idea," Cricket said. "Do you want anything from the deli? Another coffee?"

"No, I'm fine," I said as I dialed Shelby's number, and Cricket hurried toward the deli.

Once I'd spoken to Shelby about the job, I turned my attention to Toby, who was currently stalking a pretty blue butterfly. Shelby had assured me that Eden wanted to work at the bookstore and would likely stop by once she finished at the cell phone store.

When Cricket returned with her bagel and beverage, she sat down across from me. "I just can't wait until I can come and sit out here every day if I want to."

"I think it might be too cold for that in the winter," I pointed out.

"Perhaps. But if it wasn't freezing cold or wet, I'd be willing to bet the heat from the little fireplace would be enough to keep a body toasty warm."

I supposed that much might indeed be true. I'd never experienced a winter in coastal Maine, but I was willing to bet that it wasn't nearly as cold here as the winters Gus and I had shared in Northern Minnesota had been.

"So, did you get ahold of Shelby?" she asked.

"I did, and she's going to pass along my message. She's fairly certain that Eden will be by today to complete the new hire paperwork."

"She seemed really excited about the job when Nikki brought her by. Apparently, the girl actually likes to read."

I laughed. "Yes, Eden did mention that. I guess that's one of the things I liked best about her. While we both enjoyed reading a good book, neither Velma nor I would be considered prodigious readers, so having someone on staff who can make meaningful book recommendations would be very valuable."

"It is sort of funny that you bought a bookstore when you don't really like to read."

I smiled. "I guess it is a bit odd that a bookstore owner wouldn't be much of a reader, but I love this town and the people I've met, so when Vanessa offered me a reason to stay, I jumped on it. I guess you can say it was kismet."

"Ain't life grand."

Chapter 10

Velma wandered in just after noon. She apologized for being so late and explained that she'd ended up overdoing it a bit the previous evening, which had made it difficult to get out of bed this morning.

"I'm getting too old for this," she mumbled as she placed a filter in the coffee maker and began scooping in deep rich grounds.

"By *this*, do you mean late nights or too much wine?" I asked.

"Both." She reached up and plucked a mug from the rack. "I'm not usually much of a drinker, but somehow things got away from me last night. It was our first dinner party since the fire, and folks wanted to both offer condolences on the loss of the diner and congratulations on my marriage to Royce and my partnership with you at the bookstore."

"It seemed to me that there were a lot more people in attendance than you'd initially anticipated."

"A lot more," she agreed as she poured coffee into the mug. "Not that I blame Royce. I know how it is. You invite one person, but you know that the person you just invited will likely mention the dinner to a mutual friend or neighbor, so you invite the friend or neighbor as well. It doesn't take long for things to get completely out of control. Besides, this was the first dinner Royce and I had hosted since getting hitched. I guess the impromptu BBQ ended up being a second reception for those we didn't invite to the first one, which, as you know, was very small."

Velma and Royce hadn't wanted a big to-do when they finally decided to get hitched. Pastor Noah Daniels from the local church married them on the oceanfront roof of the Bistro. Shelby had decided to close the Bistro that Sunday, so the entire Bistro staff had been invited to attend. Abby and Georgia, along with the rest of the Inn at Holiday Bay crew, Marnie, Cricket, Colt, Tanner Peyton, a few others, and me were in attendance. Given the fact that Velma was one of those locals who seemed to know everyone, it wasn't surprising that the casual cookout Royce had planned had turned into something more.

"I think it's nice that the friends you weren't able to invite to the wedding were able to celebrate with you now that you're back in town." I nodded toward the closed sign on the door. "I was going to be open today but decided to stay closed. Toby and I have been working on shelving all the inventory we found in the backroom. Now that we have committed to a fairly major remodel as opposed to the tiny remodel we began with, I wanted to get the place cleaned up." I crossed my arms over my chest. "I had no idea that Vanessa was such a pack rat."

"She always kept the retail part of the bookstore looking clutter-free, but there was a lot stuffed into the rooms in the back," Velma agreed. "It will be nice to have everything freshened up a bit."

"It will be. By the way," I said as Velma refilled her mug, "I spoke to Eden and officially offered her the job on a trial basis."

"So she was still interested," Velma confirmed.

"She was. And I think she's going to work out just fine. Cricket came by this morning and had nothing but nice things to say about her, and when I spoke to Shelby, she went on and on about what a great kid she was and how if we didn't end up hiring her, she was going to create a spot for her even though she really didn't need anyone right now."

"That's good to know," Velma said. "Cricket and Shelby both have good instincts. If they think Eden will do a good job for us, I'm sure she will."

"Eden's coming in around one o'clock to complete the new hire paperwork. I figured we could talk to her about the position and ask any questions we might still have then. In the meantime, I'm going to try to get the inventory shelved."

Velma took a sip of her coffee and then set the half-empty mug on the counter. "I'll help you. I noticed that Vanessa had several boxes of mugs with the Firehouse Books logo on them stacked back in the corner. It occurred to me that we could use them in the coffee bar. Not for the to-go orders, of course, but I thought offering a beverage in a real mug rather than a paper cup would be a nice touch for those folks who want to order a coffee and pastry and sit a spell."

"I really like that idea. I hadn't noticed the mugs. If it works out, we can always order additional mugs for folks who don't mind paying extra to own one of their very own."

"If the mugs are no longer available, I'm sure we can come up with something similar. I do like the idea of having our logo out there. I found a bookstore up the coast that sells all sorts of items with their logo on them. They have some kitchen towels that I really liked, but I haven't bought them yet."

"The logo for Firehouse Books is inviting and unique. I'm sure we can think of several items that will be popular. When Wanda Anderson was in a few days ago, she had an interesting logo pen from a bookstore down the coast. Not only was the pen a real conversation piece, but the ink in the pen was bright green. It made me think of those little pens that used to be so popular when I was a kid."

"Are you talking about those little pens that were only a few inches long and came in pink, green, purple, and orange, as well as a few other colors?"

"Yes, those pens, exactly." I smiled. "I wonder if you can still get pens with all those colors."

"I suppose it might be worth looking into. It would be fun to offer logo pens in a variety of colors."

By the time Eden arrived, Velma and I had accomplished quite a lot. Toby had been sleeping on the padded window seat, which was in the sun at this time of the day, but when he heard the door open, he shot right up and hurried over to the checkout counter to welcome the newcomer.

"Hi, Toby," Eden said, bending over to pick him up and offer him a scratch behind the ear.

"He seems happy to see you," I said to the dark-haired girl.

"And I'm happy to see him." She looked in my direction. "I'm so grateful you decided to take a chance on me. I really am excited to work here and promise to do a good job."

"I'm sure you will," Velma said.

"It's a beautiful day. How about we take this paperwork and head out to the courtyard," I suggested. "You can fill it out while we chat."

"It really is a lovely day," Velma seconded.

"Okay," Eden agreed. She looked down at the kitten in her arms. "Should we bring Toby?"

"We should," I said. "I've been keeping Toby on a long leash for now. Eventually, when I'm a bit more certain that he won't wander off or follow a shopper home, I may let him wander freely, but he's still a baby, and I'm not confident that he has a good feel for the place."

"Oh, I totally agree," Eden said. "There is nothing worse than a missing pet."

It had warmed up since I'd sat out here with Cricket this morning, so I looked for a table in the shade this time. I settled Toby on his leash and offered Eden a folder with a stack of paperwork inside. It seemed that there were a lot of pages to work through, but since I'd never owned my own business and this was, in fact, my first employee, I'd just grabbed one of the new hire packets Vanessa had used. Perhaps I should have asked Velma, who had hired a lot of folks in her day, whether she thought all the forms were actually necessary.

"So tell us a bit about yourself," Velma said as Eden began to fill out the first form that asked for basic information, including items such as an address and social security number.

She looked up. "What do you want to know?"

"Where did you grow up?" Velma asked.

"Virginia."

"And did you live there until coming here?" I asked.

"No. I moved around a bit before I decided to move here. Will I need to have addresses from all my past residences?"

"No," I answered. "I was just making conversation. Knowing where a person is from can help you get a feel for them."

She paused and tilted her head as if considering this. "I guess I can understand that. As I said, I moved around a lot but lived in the town where I was born the longest. It was a small town with only a couple thousand people, and everyone was really close, and we watched out for everyone else. After moving from Virginia, I lived in lots of different places, but I missed the small-town feel I'd had as a child, so when I came here and found the town to be very similar, I decided I wanted to stay." She looked down at the form she was filling out. "I don't have a permanent address yet since I haven't found an apartment I can afford. I'm staying with Shelby and Amy while I look for a place. Should I use their address, or should I leave it blank?" Eden referred to Shelby Morris and Amy Hogan, co-owners of the Bistro.

"You can leave it blank for now," Velma suggested. "As soon as you find a place, we can fill in the blanks."

"It was really nice of Shelby to allow you to stay with her," I said.

She grinned. "She's the best. So nice and seems to be a wonderful boss. I'm really excited about working with both of you. I think a job at a bookstore suits me better than a job in food service, but if I was a waitress, Shelby would be exactly the sort of boss I'd like to have. The staff at the Bistro are a real family."

"Shelby really has created something special," Velma agreed.

"I understand you've met Marnie and Cricket, as well as the staff at the Bistro," I said.

She nodded. "Nikki introduced me to them. I understand they're moving their business to the shop across the courtyard. It will be fun to have someone closer to my age to hang out with on breaks." She blushed. "Not that the two of you are old. That isn't what I meant."

"Relax," I smiled. "Velma and I know how old we are, and while sixty-two doesn't feel old to me now that I'm here, when I was twenty-four, it would have seemed ancient."

The girl looked relieved that I wasn't angered by her comment. I could understand that. Sometimes navigating social convention was tricky.

"Nikki told me that the two of you are some of the kindest folks in Holiday Bay," Eden added. "She said that I was lucky to have found you. I know I've just met you both, but I suspect she's right."

Velma gave the girl a one-armed hug. "I think you're going to fit in here just fine."

Eden offered a genuine smile.

"Perhaps we should go over some of the specifics related to the job," I suggested.

"Okay," she agreed.

I jumped in. "Right now, we're in the process of remodeling the bookstore, so we are open random and sporadic hours. That will change once the remodel is complete and we no longer need to work around Lonnie's crew, but in the short term, I'm afraid I can't offer you set hours."

"That's fine. I'll be available when you need me and patient when you don't."

"We currently have things that you can help with which aren't sales-related," Velma joined in. "For example, we're cleaning the backroom and doing inventory as we shelve the items stored there."

"I'm happy to do anything," Eden assured us. "I understand that you have events in the evenings at times. Book clubs and that sort of thing."

I nodded. "Right now, the only evening event scheduled is the Tuesday night book club meeting, but once the remodel has been completed, we will be adding other groups. Since you actually like to read, I think that you will be a huge help with these groups."

"You should be aware, however, that the Tuesday night group is at least as much about gossip as it is about reading," Velma added.

Eden smiled. "That's fine. I like to gossip. In fact, I picked up a juicy tidbit at the Bistro when I stopped by there on my way over here."

I leaned forward slightly. "Do tell."

"Well, apparently, a woman named Virginia Danbury told Alex that she'd seen Gwen Harbinger, the woman who recently died, talking to a man named Ryan Steadman about a loan of some sort."

"Ryan Steadman is the local bank's president," I said.

"And Virginia Danbury is one of Colt's neighbors," Velma added. "In fact, I think she helps Colt by keeping an eye on Mackie and Tyler when Colt is called in to work and unable to make other arrangements. She has two sons, Adam and Andrew. I think her children are close in age to Colt's niece and nephew."

"Go on," I said, realizing that the juicy piece of gossip had likely not yet been revealed.

"Anyway, according to what I overheard, when Gwen went to the bank president about a loan to help with the mortgage, the man told Gwen that her husband had already taken out a loan against the house and that he couldn't extend the widow any additional money. Based on what Alex said to Shelby, Gwen had no idea that her husband had borrowed money against the equity in their house, and she had no idea what he'd used it for since it definitely wasn't to pay their overdue bills or repair their boat or save it from foreclosure."

"It's beginning to sound like the root of whatever is going on might be tied to the couple's financial situation," I said.

"Alex seemed to think so," Eden confirmed. "In fact, she told Shelby that she was going to have Dawson do a deep dive into the couple's finances. Alex seemed to think that Calvin might have gotten himself into something illegal. Something like drugs or gambling. She needs to research the idea further, but she mentioned to Shelby that, in her experience, when large sums of cash were unaccounted for, that sort of thing was often the reason." Eden referred to Dawson Westwood, the Bistro's bartender, bar manager, and computer whiz.

"I would think that people would have noticed if Calvin was doing drugs. Even if he had been able to fool his wife, he spent the majority of every weekday and Saturday in very close quarters with his crew," I pointed out.

"Which likely leads to a gambling addiction," Velma said.

Eden tucked a lock of hair behind her ear. "I can understand how Calvin might have gotten into trouble financially if he was gambling, and I can even understand that he might have gotten himself killed if he borrowed money from the wrong person after the money he borrowed from the bank ran out. But how did Calvin's debt result in the death of his wife? It doesn't sound like she knew anything about the gambling if, in fact, that is even what was going on."

"Without knowing a lot more about the situation, I really can't say," I said. "I guess I might try to talk to Alex later."

"I really like her," Eden said, effectively changing the topic of conversation. "Shelby introduced us, and then Shelby, Nikki, Alex, and I all had lunch together. I wasn't sure in the beginning that Holiday Bay would turn out to be as perfect as I hoped, but I already feel as if I've found a family here. It's been such a long time since I had that." She paused and looked down at her hands. "I guess I've missed that more than I realized."

"You don't have family back in Virginia?" I asked.

She paused, and I could see the hesitation in her eyes. I suspected she'd opened the door to a conversation she wasn't ready to have. Eventually, she did reply. "My mother is dead. She died when I was twelve. My father is still alive, but we don't really have a relationship."

"Do you have siblings?" I asked.

"A sister. I haven't seen her in years."

Velma and I could both see that Eden was uncomfortable talking about the past, so Velma changed the subject by asking Eden about books she'd read, and then I asked her about her skill, or lack of skill, behind the coffee counter. She didn't have any experience making coffee drinks, but she seemed more than willing to learn, and Velma seemed more than willing to teach her what she needed to know.

Eden, Velma, and I sat at the table in the shade and chatted for another hour before we decided to get back to work. I felt the three of us were bonding, and if I had to guess, we were going to make one heck of a team.

Chapter 11

Velma had plans with Royce that evening, and I didn't feel like going home to an empty house, so I decided to call Hazel and see if she wanted to come over and talk about the cat rescue and the cat lounge we'd decided to include in the bookstore's remodel. Hazel was entirely devoted to her cats, and an opportunity to have a handful of her felines showcased at the bookstore was an opportunity that I was sure she'd find too good to pass up. Since Hazel was proactive, I wasn't surprised when she happily agreed to meet with me. I suggested dinner, and she agreed that dinner would be nice. I decided to pick up takeout on my way home, and then once Hazel arrived, I'd reheat it, and we could chat while we ate. If I were honest with myself, while I was actually interested in the cat rescue, at this moment, I was even more interested in chatting with Hazel about the news Eden had shared relating to the financial situation Gwen had likely found herself in after her husband's death. Might she have willingly gotten into the car and started the engine if she'd been backed into a corner with a debt she'd never be able to dig herself out of?

"Gwen didn't commit suicide," Hazel said with a degree of certainty I didn't feel was justified.

"You seem fairly certain of this."

She leaned forward, slightly resting her elbows on the table. "Alex had the coroner take a closer look at things, and this time, they found a hallucinogen in her system."

"Hallucinogen?" I asked. "She was drugged?"

Hazel nodded. "Alex ordered a full toxicology screen, but she suspects that someone slipped something to Gwen that would have caused her to become confused and disoriented. Alex didn't have all the details when I spoke to her earlier in the day, but she did say that it appeared that Gwen was given something that would have made her compliant."

"Which is how the killer got her to obediently sit in the car while the garage filled with exhaust," I said, trying to wrap my head around the sort of drug and the drug delivery system that would cause someone to just sit there as they were slowly poisoned to death.

"That's the way it appears," Hazel confirmed.

"So, at this point, I guess the only questions are who would kill Gwen and why."

Hazel slowly nodded. "Together, those do seem to be the million-dollar question. It seems to me that Gwen's death must be related to Calvin's, but Alex admitted that she hasn't put all the pieces of this particular puzzle together yet."

I got up to refill our iced tea glasses, giving myself a moment to process everything. "If Alex is certain that Gwen was actually murdered, then I guess I have to assume that Calvin was murdered as well, but I'm still having a hard time wrapping my head around exactly what happened in that situation. Do you happen to know if Alex discovered anything new in relation to Calvin's death?"

"Not as far as I know. I know Alex has been working on it, but to this point, she hasn't found any real clues to follow. She's sure a link exists between the loan Calvin took out against the house, which he failed to tell Gwen about, and his death, but to this point, she hasn't been able to find it." She paused briefly before continuing. "The idea that Gwen was drugged makes sense to a point, but it's an idea that I'm really struggling with. I mean, who would do such a thing? The whole concept is bizarre to me."

"Are you sure that Gwen didn't take the drugs willingly? I know you feel certain that the woman hadn't killed herself, but what if she'd been addicted to drugs. What if she and Calvin both had been. Not only would that explain their financial situation, but the reason Gwen had begun to isolate as well."

Hazel didn't respond, but I could see that she was considering my idea.

"You said that Gwen had begun turning down your lunch invitations. You attributed it to money problems, which it may have been, but being addicted to mind-altering drugs would create a situation where you might begin to pull away from your friends."

Eventually, Hazel spoke. "I must admit that I will be surprised if I find out that Gwen had a drug problem, but there had been something going on. I'd noticed a change in Gwen. Not a bad change, but a change all the same. She'd seemed more energetic, and she'd lost weight. She seemed a lot perkier, yet she seemed to be run down. I asked her about it, and she told me her renewed energy and weight loss were due to her new diet and exercise program. That made sense to me, so I didn't question it, but I suppose there could have been more going on."

"Do you know if anyone else would have been in a position to notice Gwen's behavior? Perhaps a neighbor?" I asked.

"She did have a neighbor she was close to. Hannah. I guess we can ask her about Gwen's behavior. Lily wasn't in town while this was all going on, but she did seem to speak to her mother on the phone fairly often. I guess we can speak to her as well." She looked at her watch. "It isn't all that late. If you're up to it, we can drive by the Harbinger home and see if anyone is around."

I nodded. "Okay. That sounds like a good idea to me. A casual conversation with folks who likely would have noticed changes in Gwen and Calvin's behavior seems like a worthwhile errand."

Hazel decided to call Hannah to see if she was at home. Not only was Hannah home, but she was willing to speak to us. We decided to head to her place first, and then after we talked to her, we'd knock on Gwen and Calvin's door and hope that Lily was home and willing to speak to us as well. Even if Hannah was able to confirm that Gwen and Calvin had been acting oddly before their deaths, that still didn't prove they were murdered, and it certainly didn't give us a lead as to who the killer might be, but it was a place to start.

"Gwen and Calvin had both been feeling the effects of aging after having lived a hard life of physical labor," Hannah confirmed. "Calvin was the sort to take life as it came and not worry about the aches and pains he woke up with each morning, but Gwen took a much more proactive approach. In addition to the changes to her diet, she joined the gym, signed up for a yoga class, and even went to the local wellness center for acupuncture, massage, and chakra therapy." Hannah paused and then continued. "Her effort seemed to be working since she did seem to have more energy, and she managed to lose quite a bit of weight. The more promising the changes to her lifestyle were, the more involved she became in the whole fitness thing. I can't say that I know all the details relating to her transformation, but I do know that when I'd run into her as we picked up our mail or watered our lawns, she'd immediately launch into a discussion of all the cool things she had going on."

"So Gwen fully embraced this new lifestyle," Hazel said. "What about Calvin? Did he join her in her enthusiasm?"

"Not really," Hannah said. "Calvin would eat the meals Gwen prepared and even agreed to take a few of the supplements she was pushing on him. Gwen mentioned that she finally managed to get him to agree to drink the special tea she ordered and swore by. Calvin was a working man who felt he got enough exercise during the course of his day, so I don't think he was interested in going to the gym or joining any of the exercise classes Gwen was taking. I spoke to him not long before he died, and he told me that while he was trying to make Gwen happy, there was no way he was going to do anything like massage or acupuncture."

"There are folks who thought Calvin was ill before his death," I said.

She nodded. "Calvin did look pretty bad despite the change in lifestyle Gwen was forcing on him. I have a feeling he had something major going on. Heart disease or maybe cancer. Something more than the flu or a passing ailment."

"Do you know if he ever went to the doctor?" I asked.

Hannah replied. "Not that I know of. I'm not saying he didn't, but if he did, Gwen never mentioned it to me."

"Did Gwen ever mention that she and Calvin were experiencing financial issues?" Hazel asked Hannah.

She shook her head. "She didn't mention it, but I've lived in Holiday Bay a long time, so I tend to hear things. I'm not sure what was happening, but I'd heard talk about Calvin possibly losing his boat. I don't know what the couple would have done if that had occurred. It isn't as if either of them had skills they could use to start a new career at this point in their lives."

Hazel and I chatted with Hannah for a while longer, and then we knocked on the Harbingers' door in the hope of catching Lily. She didn't answer, so we headed back toward my place, where Hazel had left her car. It was a lovely summer evening that had me thinking about the beach. In fact, it was the sort of evening that made me think about romance on the beach, which was a topic I wanted to avoid at all costs.

"I spoke to Lonnie about a double-door system for the cat lounge," I grabbed the first nonromance-related thought I could think of. "He seemed to think our idea would work just fine. Velma and I have discussed putting the cat lounge in the back of the bookstore since we wanted to use the area near the bay window as a reading lounge that everyone can enjoy."

"I think that will work fine," Hazel commented as we drove back toward town. "Those interested in the cats will go into the cat lounge. It would be better if the cats were given free rein, but I understand why you need to do things the way you're planning to. There are folks who are allergic to cats, and there are likely just as many who simply aren't interested, and as a business owner, you must consider their needs."

"Keeping the cats isolated to a specific area does make the most sense," I said. "And there is the safety factor." I went on to explain about Toby getting out and how that event served as a warning that alerted me that we needed to figure out a way to ensure that none of the cats entrusted to us would end up on the street.

"I agree that ensuring the cats have a safe environment has to be the most important thing. Supervision is important as well. I spoke to Lacy, and she told me that you were planning to add an apartment over the bookstore in addition to the cat lounge and other upgrades you're doing." Hazel referred to Lacy Parker, Lonnie Parker's wife.

"I'm thinking about it," I said to Hazel. "I need to be certain that I can add all the windows I want. The space is pretty dark right now, but the views out the back will be fantastic if large windows are added."

"I guess you'll need to have an engineer come out and take a look."

"That's what Lonnie said. He's making the arrangements. Once we get the report from the engineer, Lonnie and I will discuss it further. If, for some reason, my ideas won't work, then I guess I'll need to think about finding a place."

Hazel turned in my direction. "The house Vanessa owns that you're currently staying in is nice, and I understand that she plans to sell it."

"It is a nice house, and Vanessa does plan to put it on the market, but I think I'd like something smaller. It's just Toby and me, and we don't need nearly the square footage Vanessa's house has. Besides, if I live above the bookstore, you won't have to transport the rescue cats we feature back and forth between the bookstore and the sanctuary. I figure that if I'm going to host four or five cats at a time, they can just come upstairs with Toby and me at the end of the day."

"That would be helpful," she agreed as we parked in the driveway and headed inside. After we were inside, Hazel glanced at the kitten, who was napping at the top of the tower I'd purchased for him. "Toby seems to have settled in. I hate to even bring this up on the off chance I might be reading things wrong, but should I assume I no longer need to look for someone to foster him?"

I smiled. "Toby is here to stay. I suppose you likely knew that would be the case all along. Velma told me that you are somewhat famous for asking potential cat parents for a short-term favor, all the while hoping that something permanent will work out."

She chuckled. "I guess I should probably admit that I've used this strategy a time or two. Most times, it works out just fine, and the cats in my care end up being happy with the humans I've selected for them."

"It's nice that you care about them so much. We had strays in Minnesota, but more often than not, they ended up as barn cats for anyone willing to feed them. It's nice that you care enough about the cats to give them a real chance at a home and family."

Hazel and I continued talking about the cats and the rescue that was near and dear to her heart. I had a feeling that the two of us were likely to become good friends the same way Velma and I had. When I came to Holiday Bay, I'd hoped to find a distraction from the hopelessness I couldn't quite shake after my husband's death. It seemed I'd found what I was looking for, but the blessings I hadn't been expecting were considerable. I'd had friends in Minnesota, but the people I'd been the closest to were "couple friends" with Gus and me. After he was gone, our friends tried to be there for me, but being around them left me feeling empty inside. In Holiday Bay, I had friends who belonged just to me. I loved the people I'd left behind and planned to stay in touch with them, but knowing that I had a new family that seemed to match my new life had gone a long way toward helping me feel whole again.

Chapter 12

Velma, Eden, and I all arrived for work early Monday morning. Our plan was to try to maintain somewhat regular hours despite all the construction that was going on. Lonnie and his men were making good progress on the coffee bar addition, and the other minor changes I'd spoken to Lonnie about were moving along nicely. In addition to the sectioned-off cat lounge, Lonnie suggested an outdoor component, or cattery, that could be further sectioned off and closed during the winter. I liked the idea in concept but wanted to see a drawing to get a feel for exactly what we were looking at. Lonnie agreed to draw up plans for my consideration and indicated that we could discuss the project at some point during the week.

The engineer was coming to look at my apartment project this week. Initially, I'd been told that the man was booking appointments more than a month out, but Lonnie called in a favor, and the engineer had assured him that he'd find time to stop by within the next day or two.

"Do you want me to reshelve the books you removed from the stacks while the contractors were here last week?" Eden asked.

"I think Lonnie's men are about done in that area, so reshelving the books should be fine," I answered. "You'll need to dust all the shelves and vacuum the area really well before beginning the reshelving process."

"I'm already on it," Eden said, and it appeared she was.

I had to admit I really enjoyed the girl's enthusiasm and energy. It seemed I awoke most mornings feeling even more tired and achy than when I'd gone to bed. I supposed that achy joints were part of the aging process, but I didn't remember it taking quite so long to get going in the mornings before Gus passed away. Of course, I had a good reason to get up early when Gus was alive. The man loved his breakfast. Bacon and eggs most mornings, with occasional waffles piled high with butter and syrup. Gus had an active metabolism, so he never gained weight as he aged, but looking back over the types of meals we generally enjoyed, I could see how they most likely had contributed to his heart attack. Since Gus had been gone, my appetite was nearly nonexistent. Or at least it had been. Lately, it seemed that my appetite and energy were slowly making their way back, and the weight I'd lost after Gus had died was most definitely making a comeback as well. I was a petite woman, who couldn't handle much extra weight, so I supposed I needed to start keeping my eye on the situation. I could see how Gwen could have become completely immersed in her new lifestyle if, in fact, the diet, supplement, and exercise routine she'd mapped out had been working as well as Hannah made it sound.

In Minnesota, I'd shoveled snow in the winter and worked in the yard in the summer. So far, I'd done neither during my stay in Holiday Bay. Velma had mentioned that she might be interested in joining the new gym just outside of town now that she wasn't spending her days on her feet at the diner. Perhaps I'd go along with her if she actually decided to check it out. I'd never had the need for exercise outside of work or recreation, but since my energy output had changed dramatically since moving to Maine, I supposed it was important that my lifestyle change with my new circumstances.

"I'm thinking about offering daily coffee specials," Velma said as she stood back and looked at the chalkboard she'd just hung on the wall behind the coffee counter. "That will require that we buy a variety of specialty syrups. Likely more than we would if we only offered the basics. But I think a different coffee special each day would be fun and might persuade folks to come in more often."

"I love caramel," Eden said.

"I've always been a fan of pumpkin in the fall and peppermint during the Christmas holidays," I added.

"I have a recipe for a boysenberry iced coffee that I think will be a hit in the summer," Velma informed me.

I nodded. "I think a daily coffee special will be fun. Perhaps we can do a pastry special to go along with it."

"Like a triple berry muffin with a boysenberry iced coffee," Eden suggested.

"Exactly like that," I agreed. "By the way," I added since we were discussing the coffee counter, "I spoke to Vanessa, and she gave me the contact information for the vendor she bought the Firehouse Books coffee mugs from. She wasn't sure if they were still in business, but I thought I'd call them later. After thinking about what you said about having mugs to sell to folks, I really like the idea. In fact," I continued, "I also like our idea to add souvenir-type items to our inventory. Nothing gaudy, of course, but specialty items that represent the bookstore and the area we live in."

"Like firehouse salt and pepper shakers," Eden suggested.

"Perhaps. I guess the first step should be to see what sort of items are available at a reasonable cost and then figure it out from there."

"You know," Eden said, "in addition to souvenir items with a firehouse theme to go with the name of the bookstore or items that would complement the seaside location of the bookstore, such as a lighthouse or seashells, we might also want to offer items with a cat theme. We could donate a percentage of the proceeds from these items to the cat sanctuary."

I smiled at the girl. "That's an excellent idea."

"We'd need to talk to someone about the feasibility of keeping track of the items we designate as fundraising items from the general inventory, but I like the idea as well," Velma said.

Toby wandered over, and I picked him up. He sure was a cute little thing. I had a feeling that he was going to enjoy having other cats to play with once we started accepting the rescues. Hazel had assured me that she would only bring rescue cats and kittens to the bookstore who'd been checked by a veterinarian and had received all their shots. I appreciated that since I wanted to be sure I kept Toby safe from outside illnesses.

"Did you ever order those paperbacks we talked about?" Velma asked.

"I called and left a message for the saleswoman. Her voicemail indicated that she'd get back to me today." I looked at my cell phone, which began to chime, indicating I had a call. "I suspect that may be her now. "Good morning, this is Lou," I answered.

"Hey, darlin'."

My heart skipped a beat. "Tuck?" I asked as I tried to make sense of the voice on the other end of the line.

"Surprised to hear from me?"

Now that was an understatement. "It's been a while." *Nearly forty years*, I thought to myself, but I didn't say as much.

"I guess it has been a while, but you know that choice wasn't mine. You told me to go, so I went."

I guess that much, at least, was true.

"I was sorry to hear about Gus," he added, in a tone that sounded genuine.

"Thank you," I whispered. "It was all very sudden."

"Sometimes that's the way these things go. Doesn't make it any easier, but I am happy he didn't suffer."

"I agree," I said, although sometimes I wished we would have had the chance to say our goodbyes. I liked to think I hadn't left a lot unsaid, but when the person you love most in the world goes from seeming fairly healthy to being gone in an instant, it causes you to wonder what might have been.

"I heard you moved to Holiday Bay, Maine," Tuck continued.

"Yes. I'm not sure if you remember my niece, Vanessa."

"Of course, I remember Vanessa. How is she?"

I put a hand to my chest in an effort to slow my racing heart. "Vanessa's good. She moved to Italy."

"Did she now? Good for her. Vanessa always was the adventurous sort."

Actually, until this recent totally impulsive move on Vanessa's part, she hadn't been adventurous at all.

I continued. "Anyway, after Vanessa decided to move, I purchased the bookstore she owned, which prompted the move to Maine. Are you still in Minneapolis?"

"Actually, I live in Maine now as well."

"You don't say," I choked out. Tucker Carlson was the one who got away. The one I still sometimes dreamt of. The one who, if not for my Gus, I'd likely have married. "Northern Maine?" I asked with much more hope in my voice than would be considered polite since Holiday Bay hugged the shoreline on the southeastern edge of the state.

He chuckled. "Bar Harbor, actually."

Bar Harbor was too close. Much, much too close for this current complication.

"I decided to retire to the area after I sold my business," he added.

"That's great," my voice sounded high and screechy despite my best effort to keep it level. "That's great. Really, really great." I hoped he didn't hear the panic in my tone. "Are you retired or doing something else?"

"Retired."

Tuck continued to speak, but I wasn't really listening. Once upon a time, I'd loved two men and had been forced to choose one. It should have been an easy choice since by the time Tuck came wandering into my life, Gus and I were already an item, but it wasn't. Looking back, I realized that if not for the fact that my mother was best friends with Gus's mother and the two women had been planning our wedding since before we were even dating, I'd have likely chosen Tuck. Not that I hadn't loved Gus. He'd been a good guy who was well-liked and respected. He'd been honest, hardworking, and dependable. Everyone had assured me that he'd make me happy.

"I thought that since we both ended up in the same corner of the world, we could have dinner. Maybe catch up," Tuck suggested.

I wanted to politely find a way to decline, but for some reason, I froze. Dinner with Tuck? Should I even go there? Gus had loved me, and I'd loved him. We'd had a wonderful life together, and I'd tried never to look back once I'd made my choice. Gus and I had talked about the inevitability of one of us surviving the other during one of our heart-to-heart conversations, so I knew that Gus would want me to move on now that he was gone. Still, even with that knowledge, I also knew he would prefer I move on with literally any man on earth other than Tuck Carlson.

Out of the corner of my eye, I noticed the odd look Velma was sending me and realized that I must have paused a bit too long. I quickly commented that I was at work and needed to get back. He made a comment about me having his number, and then he rang off by saying that he hoped I'd call.

"Is everything okay?" Velma asked after I hung up.

"No, not really."

"Do you want to talk about it?" she asked.

I just stared at her, finding myself unable to compose a proper response to her offer.

"Do you want me to go?" Eden asked.

I turned and smiled at her. "No, sweetheart. You're fine. I'm fine. I guess the call just threw me." I paused as I tried to figure out what more to say. "That was an old friend I haven't heard from in forty years."

"That's a long time," Eden said.

"It is," I agreed, remembering long nights of agony trying to decide which man to keep and which to send away. "A lifetime," I added, even as I admitted to myself that, in some ways, it seemed like just yesterday.

I noticed that Velma stared at me with a contemplative expression on her face, but thankfully, when she spoke, it was to ask about the bookmarks we'd discussed ordering at the same time I'd ordered our last shipment of note cards. I was happy for the distraction, which made my voice much too animated and sing-songy for the ordinary conversation we were having, but after a lengthy explanation relating to the pros and cons of the three companies I'd narrowed things down to, we made our choice, and I somehow merged back into my day.

Tuck Carlson! I thought to myself as I began sorting and then resorting that same pile of receipts. I'd be lying to myself if I didn't admit that Tuck had once meant a lot to me, but he was really nothing more than a blast from my past, and I suspected I'd be better off not getting tangled up with the man all over again.

"I entered those receipts into the ledger this morning," Velma informed me.

I looked down at the pile of cash register slips that had started off as neatly stacked but were now a mess. "Thank you. I didn't realize you'd gotten around to it."

She smiled at me, and I looked down at my hands. Suddenly, I had no idea what to do with them. Deciding I needed some air, I headed toward the back door, which led out into the courtyard. Finding a seat in the shade, I found myself wishing that I'd never quit smoking. I'd given it up thirty years ago and rarely missed it, but at this moment, smoking would have given me something to do other than obsess over what might have been.

I leaned my head back, closed my eyes, and pictured Tuck with his crooked smile and long dark hair. He'd likely be gray now. I put a hand on my long white hair and wondered if Tuck would even recognize me if we happened to run into each other on the street. I was reasonably sure I'd recognize his deep blue eyes anywhere, but eye color faded as surely as hair turned first gray and then white, so perhaps the eyes I remembered wouldn't be the eyes I'd see when I looked at him now.

Tuck Carlson, I thought to myself as I pictured the free-spirited man who'd loved the open road as much as I had. I wondered if he still rode that old Harley of his. Probably not. The bike was on its last leg forty years ago, so I doubted it'd still run today. Of course, Tuck was an excellent mechanic, so perhaps he'd refurbished it. He used to talk about doing exactly that once he'd saved the cash he'd need for the parts.

I glanced back toward the bookstore as Velma crossed the courtyard in my direction. She looked hesitant, so I motioned her over. "It sure is lovely today," I said conversationally. My mama always told me that when in need of a safe conversation starter, the weather was the one subject that couldn't be beaten.

"I hear that the high temperature is supposed to top out at nearly eighty today," Velma said, doing her best I was sure to help me fill the awkwardness of a quiet moment.

I had to laugh as the absurdity of our conversation really hit me. Velma laughed as well. Eventually, she spoke. "I came out to let you know that the saleswoman you wanted to order the new paperbacks from is on the phone."

"I should talk to her." I stood up. "I'm struggling with the choice in format for some of the less popular books. Do I order everything in hardback, or should I wait for the paperback version to be released?"

"I like a hardback," Velma said. "But with everything being offered in eBook format for a fraction of the price, hardcover books have become less popular."

I walked back into the bookstore, and Velma followed me. I allowed myself to forget about Tuck and focus on the brilliance of this very ordinary moment. Getting together with Tuck was tempting, but hadn't I just been thinking that what I really needed in my life were more ordinary moments? During the months that Tuck and I had been together, I was fairly certain that not a single moment we shared could in any way be classified as ordinary.

Chapter 13

"Maybe you can go on a picnic," Eden suggested, seemingly from out of nowhere, after I ordered the paperbacks and hung up.

"Picnic?" I said, glancing at her with what I was sure was a look of confusion.

Eden turned red. "I'm sorry, I guess my comment was delayed to the point where it no longer makes sense. What I meant was that maybe you and your friend from your earlier conversation should go on a picnic and catch up." She blushed an even deeper color. "Although, I just realized that perhaps it isn't my place to offer a suggestion. I didn't mean to listen in, but I could hear what he was saying when he was talking." She put her hands over her face.

I reached out a hand and touched her arm. "It's okay. Tuck does have a loud voice. Very commanding. I used to kid him about the volume of his voice announcing his presence long before he came into view."

"So you were close?" Eden asked.

I nodded. "We were. Once upon a time. But like I said, it's been a long time."

I hadn't seen Tuck since the day that he'd walked out of my life. The decision to let him go was the hardest decision I'd ever made in my life, and after I'd made it, I'd never spoken to him again. I didn't write to him or follow his movements as he traveled from one place to another. I wasn't sure about the details of his life, but I heard from a cousin who knew us both that while Tuck had lived a full and meaningful life, he'd never married.

"I heard that Alex had a nice long chat with Gibson Long," Velma said, seeming once again to rescue me by changing the subject.

"Who's Gibson Long?" Eden asked, thankfully becoming pulled in by a topic of conversation more intriguing than my ancient love life.

"Gibson Long is, or I guess I should say was, a close friend of Calvin Harbinger's," Velma explained. "Gibson and Calvin were friends for a long time, and most would say they knew each other well, but something happened between the men about a year ago. I can't say I know with any degree of certainty what came between the men, but I will say that it has been my experience that friendships such as the one the two men shared don't usually fall apart unless there's a really good reason."

"Like a woman," Eden said.

"Exactly like a woman," Velma agreed.

"I thought Gwen and Calvin had been happily married," I said, even though I'd never met either the wife or the husband.

"They got along okay, but I wouldn't say they were happy," Velma said. "They seemed to work because they'd committed to making it work. On the surface, I suppose they may have even appeared happy, but if you really paid attention, it was hard to miss the apathy that seemed to lie beneath the façade they presented to the world. I'm not saying that Calvin cheated, mind you," Velma said with conviction. "I'm just saying that something went on between Calvin and Gibson, and if I were to find out that the something that destroyed their friendship was a woman, I wouldn't be surprised. You know how messy love can be."

Boy, didn't I.

"So are you saying that Calvin might have made a move on his best friend's girl?" Eden asked.

"I'm saying it's a possibility. Calvin had been married to the same woman for a long time, and given their seeming lack of any real passion, I guess I can see how he might have wandered. Gibson had been divorced almost as long as Calvin had been married and tended to date a lot. I suppose it might be possible that Calvin developed feelings for Gibson's current love interest, which might have been enough to end the relationship."

"But you don't know if any of this is for sure, right?" Eden asked Velma.

"No, I don't know any of this for sure. In fact, all I did was make up a story that might or might not fit the narrative."

I wasn't sure whether Velma actually thought Calvin might have cheated or if she'd simply made up a juicy story to divert Eden from her interest in my tale of love gone wrong. But if Calvin and his best friend were actually on the outs, I supposed it was a piece of information that seemed relevant enough to follow up on.

"I noticed that the new gym in town has a coupon in the newspaper," Velma said, changing the subject once again. "I thought I'd go by and check it out. I'm still not sure that exercise classes are quite right for me, but I can see myself riding the bikes or strolling on a treadmill a couple times a week."

"I heard that place has saunas and Jacuzzis," Eden informed us. "A couple of the waitresses at the Bistro joined so they could head over after work and relax after their shift."

"I wouldn't mind using the sauna occasionally," I said. "I'm not sure about the rest of it, but I'm going to need to do something to get some exercise now that I no longer have a garden to tend to. Maybe the weights. They seem to be more my style than some of the other offerings." I looked at Velma. "Maybe the two of us should stop by this afternoon after we close for the day. I don't suppose it would hurt to take a look."

"Sounds good to me. Royce bowls on Mondays, so I won't be in a hurry to get home. Maybe we could even grab a bite to eat after."

I was about to ask Eden if she wanted to come with us when she informed us that she had plans with Nikki, who was off today. Nikki and Eden planned to head out to the inn to hang out with Haven, who was younger than they were but with whom they shared similar interests.

"It's nice that you've become friends with Nikki and Haven," I said to Eden.

"They really are the best. Nikki is so much fun, and she's lived here long enough that she knows everyone and can fill me in on who's who. And Haven and I have a lot in common, so I feel like she really gets me. I think Haven is happy to have someone in her life with a similar background as well."

"Did you grow up in the same area?" I asked.

"Actually, we are both from Virginia, but having a common birth state isn't what I was referring to. I think I feel close to her because we both spent time in foster care and ran away before we were eighteen. I won't say our histories are exactly alike, but they are eerily close to being the very same."

I hadn't realized that Eden had been in foster care or that she'd run away before turning eighteen until this moment. She was twenty-four now, so I supposed all that didn't matter, but I was curious. I knew Haven had lost her family in a house fire when she was only twelve. Haven managed to escape through a window and ran to a neighbor's house for help, but it was too late for her family. She was put in foster care but never really settled. When she was fifteen, she ran away from her foster home. She showed up at the inn when she was seventeen, and Abby and Georgia took her in. She was eighteen now and had settled right in quite nicely.

"I didn't realize you'd been in foster care," I said carefully. I figured if Eden wanted to talk about it, I'd give her an opening, and if she didn't, I'd let it go.

She shrugged. "It was a long time ago. Should I put books on those little shelves behind the cash register, or are you planning on adding decorative items?"

Okay. It sounded as if Eden wasn't ready to talk yet, which was fine. I knew how these sorts of things went. "I think I'd like to use those little shelves to display items we may be featuring or have on sale. I also thought the shelves would be a good place to display seasonal items we might want to change each month."

Eden nodded but didn't respond.

"Were you able to speak to Lily as you'd planned to do this weekend?" Velma asked me, changing the subject yet again.

"No," I answered. "Hazel and I went by the house, but she wasn't home. Hazel planned to try again. I'm not sure if she was able to connect. I guess

I'll have to ask her. I assume you never made it by to speak to her either."

"No, I didn't," Velma confirmed. "Maybe we can stop by later this afternoon."

"I've never met Lily personally, but Kennedy knows Lily, and she mentioned to Shelby while I was close enough to overhear that Lily visited a friend for the weekend," Eden shared. "Kennedy said that she was having a difficult time dealing with the stress of losing her parents and was feeling overwhelmed with having to take care of things on her own. Lily told Kennedy she hoped her older brother would show up this week and help her, but Kennedy didn't seem confident that he would." Eden referred to Kennedy Swanson, a long-time employee of the Bistro and single mother.

"It is unfortunate that the girl doesn't have the help she needs," I said.

"I'm going to call Hazel and see what she knows," Velma informed us. "Maybe there's something we can do to help Lily in the absence of available family."

Velma went into the office to make her call while Eden and I continued to unpack boxes. Vanessa had stored a lot of really cute items away that she really should have offered for sale long before this, but she'd also stored a bunch of junk that would need to be hauled away. Until I'd spent time in the bookstore, I hadn't been aware that Vanessa was such a hoarder. Of course, in the past, Vanessa had usually traveled to Minnesota to visit me rather than me traveling to

Holiday Bay to visit her, so my exposure to the bookstore had been limited.

"Hazel is going to stop by the house this morning to check on Lily," Velma informed us. "She'll call after she stops by whether she makes contact or not."

"I guess we've done what we can," I said once Velma had shared her news. "It looks like Lonnie just pulled into the parking area. Maybe he'll have an update for us."

Chapter 14

As it turned out, Lonnie did have an update, which I fully welcomed since he'd come by to inform us that he'd hired some extra laborers and that if we could allow him full access to the bookstore for two weeks, he could get the whole thing done, including the cat lounge. It would be nice to just be done with it, so I agreed to be closed for the time he needed beginning tomorrow, and he agreed to line up everything he needed in order to finish the job in the least amount of time. Of course, Lonnie wouldn't be able to begin the remodel on my second-floor apartment until the engineer came out to evaluate the feasibility of making the changes I wanted. Lonny assured me, however, that once we got the go-ahead, he'd make the necessary arrangements to get that part of the job done efficiently as well.

Once Lonnie and I had discussed all my remodeling projects, he informed me that he had a job to finish up that afternoon, so he could start on my job full-time the following day. Since it was a gorgeous day, I decided to walk him out to his truck. He was pulling out of the parking lot when Hazel pulled in. I waved and then waited for her to park.

"Oh good, you're here," she said after sliding into a spot near where I was standing and rolling her window down. "I tried calling, but you didn't answer your cell phone."

"I'm sorry. I guess I left my cell phone on my desk. I've been chatting with Lonnie about the remodel. Is something going on?"

She nodded. "It's Lily. I stopped to check on her and found her acting quite oddly."

"Oddly?" I asked. "What do you mean by that?"

"Confused. At first, I thought Lily was drunk, but she wasn't acting drunk. She wasn't stumbling around or anything like that, but it seemed like she was in a daze. Lily would start a sentence and then just leave it dangling. She got up at one point to refill the tea she was drinking, but after walking into the kitchen, she just stood there. It was as if she couldn't remember what she was supposed to be doing."

I laughed. "I guess that's happened to me more often than I care to admit."

Hazel smiled back. "It's happened to me as well, but Lily is in her twenties and not her sixties. She's usually a lively sort, but when I went to speak to her today, she just seemed flat. I'm not sure I can explain it. I thought about calling Alex or maybe even calling for medical assistance, but she seemed to shake it off and assured me she was fine. I was hoping you had the time and would be willing to visit Lily with me and see what you think. At this point, a second opinion would be welcome. I hate to start calling in emergency personnel if the girl actually is perfectly okay as she insists she is."

I shrugged. "Okay. I'll go to Lily's house with you. I can't say that I know a lot about this sort of behavior pattern, but I do agree that it never hurts to get a second opinion. I'll ask Velma to come as well. She's been trying to get ahold of Lily, but I guess she was out of town this past weekend."

Eden agreed to keep an eye on Toby while she continued to work on shelving merchandise, so Velma and I left with Hazel. When we arrived at Lily's, I immediately understood why Hazel was concerned. The woman greeted us at the door and invited us in. She started to walk toward the main living area, which was at the back of the house, but then she just stopped. She didn't say anything or attempt to change directions. She just stood there. Velma took her by the arm and suggested that we talk in the family room, and she nodded and allowed Velma to lead her to the sofa. Once we were seated, Hazel asked her how she felt, and she said okay. Hazel went into the kitchen and poured a glass of water for Lily. She brought it back into the seating area and handed it to her. Lily lifted the glass halfway to her mouth and just stopped.

"I think she may have had a stroke," I said. "I think we should take her to the hospital."

"I agree," Velma said, looking at Lily. "Lily, honey, Hazel, Lou, and I are going to take you to see the doctor."

Lily just stared at Velma as if trying to make sense of what she was saying.

"Should we bring the baby?" she asked.

Hazel glanced at me. I shrugged.

"What baby?" Velma asked.

She looked around, frowned, and then just stared at the wall.

Once Hazel, Velma, and I helped her into the car, we headed to the hospital. The doctor talked to Lily and then decided to admit her so he could do some tests. He agreed that it was possible that Lily had a stroke but that he thought it was more likely that some sort of drug interaction was responsible for Lily's odd behavior. There didn't seem to be a reason for us to stay at the hospital. The doctor assured us that he would likely keep her overnight and would call whoever we left as a contact once he had a better idea of what was going on.

I was afraid Lily would be frightened when we left, but she seemed really out of it. She just stared at the wall, devoid of any emotional response.

"Lily is so young. It would be tragic if she suffered a medical event that left her permanently disabled," I said.

"I am concerned," Hazel said. "Gwen never said anything about Lily being into drugs, but I guess she might have taken something to help deal with her anxiety."

"It does seem that everyone who has spoken to her since she's been home has commented on her elevated stress level," Velma agreed.

"The comment about the baby was odd, though," Hazel said. "I get how an unfortunate combination of drugs might cause confusion and an inability to focus, but the whole thing with the baby made it seem like she was hallucinating."

"I guess she may have been," I agreed. "Or maybe she'd seen a baby earlier and simply didn't remember that she'd left wherever it was she'd seen the baby and was home."

Velma turned and looked in my direction. "We're not all that far from the gym. As long as we're out, should we stop by and see what they have to offer?"

I looked at Hazel. "Do you mind stopping?"

"Not at all," she answered. "I've been meaning to check the place out for a while now."

I still wasn't sure that a gym environment would work for me, but I did need to do something, so I agreed that now was as good a time as any.

Chapter 15

The gym was actually very nice. Everything was clean and new, and positive energy flowed through the facility. The background music was upbeat without being overpowering, and the layout made sense from a user standpoint. Many group classes were currently in session, so the majority of the rooms used for that purpose were occupied. I poked my head into a few of the rooms before following our guide down the hallway to the area that housed the weights as well as the aerobic machines, such as stationary bikes and treadmills. The stair climber actually looked fun, as did the ski machine. I'd planned to focus on the weights almost exclusively, but maybe I'd step out of my comfort zone since I'd be paying for an all-access pass if I decided to join.

"Now that you've seen the main workout areas, I'd like to take you back to the locker rooms," our guide said. "There are saunas and Jacuzzis in both the men's and the women's areas. Lockers are provided to our members free of charge, and the showers are large and always clean." She opened the door to a room with the Jacuzzis.

It really was quite pleasant. I was pretty sure the potted palm trees were fake, but they provided the illusion of a luxury vacation. Given the fact that it was toasty warm in the room, I could see this would be a nice place to hang out in the winter.

"The juice and supplement bars are located beyond the double doors in the back. While many of our members prefer to follow the diet they always have, our juice cleanses are becoming increasingly popular. In addition to juice, we offer a variety of products that will optimize your health, including powders, pills, and specialty teas."

"About the teas," I began. "Do any of your teas provide a mellowing effect?"

"We do have teas to help with both sleep and stress. Are you interested in such a product?"

"Not really," I answered. "But before Gwen Harbinger passed away, she spoke quite a lot about a special tea she'd been drinking that she felt both improved her health and helped her to lose weight."

The woman frowned. "I'm afraid that while Gwen was a member and worked out with us, she purchased her supplements and teas elsewhere. Some of our members prefer to do things that way, but if you decide to go that route, I want to caution you that while our products are tested and approved by the medical community, not all of these types of products go through the same vetting process. Gwen was getting at least some of the products she was using from international sources that aren't necessarily put through the same safety testing. I wouldn't recommend going that route. There's been a lot of press as of late as to how dangerous some of these products can be."

"Could a product such as the ones Gwen likely used have caused confusion?" Velma asked.

"Sure," the perky brunette said. "I've heard stories about folks walking into the middle of a busy highway while under the influence of certain teas. I guess there are some tea blends that have a hypnotic effect and are often used to achieve a state of deep meditation. Some of these blends can even cause hallucinations, which I personally think sounds awful, but there are certain religious ceremonies that work best when those who participate are deep in an altered state of consciousness. But unless you're going to participate in such a ceremony, I wouldn't recommend going there. These teas can be dangerous."

"It does sound like it might be best to avoid those sorts of blends altogether," Velma agreed.

I glanced at Hazel. Her eyes were narrowed, and her brow furrowed. I suspected that she'd caught onto the intent of Velma's line of questioning. Could Gwen, and perhaps even Calvin, actually have died while under the influence of the tea Gwen seemed to be hooked on? It seemed to me that if people under the influence had actually walked into traffic without even realizing what they were doing, then getting in their car, starting their ignition, and then forgetting what they were doing might be possible as well.

After leaving the gym with a promise to our guide to talk it over and get back to her, Hazel, Velma, and I headed toward Hazel's car.

"Do you think Gwen died while under the influence of the tea?" Hazel asked.

I nodded. "It occurred to me that might be a possibility. Gwen seemed to have been really into the tea, and everyone said she'd been acting oddly. After seeing Lily's behavior for myself this morning, it's occurred to me that Gwen's death actually could have been a horrible accident."

Velma frowned. "So are we saying Gwen drank some of the tea and then decided to go somewhere? She enters the garage, gets in her car, starts the engine, and then spaces out and forgets what she is doing?"

"I suppose that if she was out of it enough, she might have just sat there while she was slowly poisoned by the carbon monoxide," Hazel agreed.

The idea really did make a whole lot of sense.

"The thing is," Hazel added, "Gwen has been drinking the tea for months. If the tea had that sort of effect, wouldn't it have been apparent before now?"

"What if there was something different about the current batch of tea?" I asked. "Perhaps Gwen bought tea from another vendor, or the usual strength she'd been using was no longer working, so she decided to get something stronger."

"Okay," Hazel said. "That makes sense to a point, but how do we prove it?"

"Lily was drinking tea this morning," Velma said. "I think we can assume the tea Lily consumed is the same tea Gwen drank. We have the tea and can have it tested. Lily's already at the hospital, so it shouldn't be all that hard to have a toxicology screen done that will test for elements that might be found in the tea. The doctor should be able to tell us if the ingredients included in the tea would cause behavior such as that being exhibited by Lily."

"And if we can determine that Lily's behavior was caused by the tea, then we should be able to make a general statement about how the tea might have affected Gwen on the day she died."

"What about Calvin?" I asked.

Hazel shrugged. "It seemed as if he simply fell into the sea and was rendered unable to get back onboard his boat. His body has been cremated, and I doubt they screened for elements that would be found in the tea. I suppose we could make a case that if the tea could, in fact, cause hallucinations when consumed in a large enough quantity, then Calvin might have been drinking the same tea when he died, which caused him to see something in the water that caused him to jump in."

"Or something in the boat that he wanted to escape. Something that wasn't actually there."

It seemed that Hazel and I had a theory as to what might have been behind the deaths of Gwen and her husband. It was a good theory, but we would need some sort of proof. I supposed finding that proof was our next challenge.

Chapter 16

By the following day, Hazel had spoken to Lily's doctor, who confirmed that her odd behavior had likely been the direct result of drinking an excessive quantity of the tea Lily had found in her mother's pantry. The tea contained herbs that could potentially relax an individual who consumed a large amount of the blend almost to the point of paralysis. In addition to the herbs, other ingredients, such as peyote, a known hallucinogen, were present in the tea. The doctor assured Hazel that Lily should be fine now that the effects had worn off.

Hazel had asked the doctor if he thought an overdose of the tea in Gwen's system might have caused her to get into her car, start the engine, and then forget why she was there. The doctor said that while he didn't have any evidence to offer that would prove that this was what had happened, it did at least seem possible to him that the behavior I described could have occurred if she'd consumed enough of the tea. I brought up the fact that Gwen had been drinking the tea for months, and the doctor shared that the tea wouldn't necessarily have the effect it seemed to have had on Lily if it was consumed in small quantities. If drinking the tea caused Gwen's death, then it was likely that she'd consumed more than usual on the day she died.

Between the hallucinogenic effect of the peyote and the calming effect of the interaction of some of the other ingredients, Lily's doctor was likewise willing to state that it was at least a possibility that Calvin, had he drank enough of the tea, could have jumped into the water either in response to something he thought he saw in the water, or in order to escape something he thought he saw on the boat. Calvin could have become confused and disoriented once he was in the water and was rendered unable to get back onboard.

Hazel and I stopped at the police station and shared our theory with Alex. She admitted that the theory made sense, although it did seem nearly impossible that we'd be able to prove any of it one way or the other. Without a witness to either death, all we were really left with were theories.

At least Lily was going to be okay. The doctor had confirmed that there wouldn't be any long-term effects from her ordeal and then released her. Once Lily entered her parents' home, she immediately washed what was left of her mother's tea and supplement collection down the drain. The local newspaper was alerted about the effects of the herbs and other ingredients found in the tea and published an article warning the residents of our community to be aware of the potential risks of buying those sorts of items from sources that weren't subjected to the same safety standards as similar items purchased from reputable companies.

"It's a bit aggravating that we can't prove any of this," I commented to Hazel. "I suppose I'll just be happy that Lily turned out to be okay and that her experience has brought awareness of the issue to the community."

"I think that's all we can do," Hazel agreed.

"Colt has been doing this a long time, and he'd be the first one to tell you that there are a lot of cases that can't be solved without a shadow of a doubt," Velma shared.

"When is Colt coming back anyway?" Hazel asked.

"Not until next week," Velma answered.

"I'll be happy to have him back," I said, "but I think Alex has been doing a fantastic job in his absence."

Velma and Hazel agreed that was true. Not only had Alex followed up on Gwen's death as she'd promised she would, but she'd located Bradley Boxer, the missing teen, who, as she predicted, had ended up being a runaway teen all along.

Hazel headed home after dropping me off at the bookstore. Velma and I went back to work clearing out the storage area. I loved the idea of having the remodel done in time for the autumn leaf season and was already thinking of ways I could decorate. It felt good to feel a spark of something resembling anticipation. It had been a while since I'd wanted to think about or plan for any moment beyond the one I was currently living.

"Hey, everyone," Eden greeted Velma and me as she entered the bookstore through the front door. "I know we're closed today since Lonnie and his crew are working on the remodel, but I wondered if a decision had been made about canceling tonight's book club meeting. Shelby asked me about it, and I realized I had no idea if we were still on or not."

"I wouldn't mind meeting," I said.

"I'm in as well," Velma seconded. "I spoke to Alice Farthington, and she shared how much she enjoyed the easy companionship she's found with the group. I think gatherings such as ours are an important step in her recovery from the grief she must still be dealing with."

"I think the meeting helped Alice even more than you might realize," Eden said.

"Perhaps we should call the regulars and let them know what we're doing," I suggested. "I'm sure that a lot of folks will be wondering what our plans are, given the fact that the store was closed today."

"I don't mind making the calls if you have a list," Eden offered.

I agreed that would be a perfect job for her and printed a list of contacts with current cell numbers from my computer. "I don't have a cell number for Savannah. I'm not sure if she's even in town, so you should ask Georgia about it when you speak to her since she mentioned that she'd be interested in attending."

"Okay. Is there anyone else I should specifically seek out?"

I glanced at the list. "Gabby from the police station isn't on the list, and while Alex didn't come last week, she did mention that she enjoyed reading, so let's invite her as well. You might want to start with Marnie and Cricket. They often have someone in mind that they'd like to invite."

"If they ask about snacks, let them know I have it handled this week," Velma said.

Eden nodded. "Is it okay if I invite Haven? I don't know if she'll be able to come, but Nikki mentioned the group to her a few days ago, and she seemed interested."

"She'd be a welcome addition," I said. It did my heart good to see my community of friends expanding. Gus and I had enjoyed a lot of friends when he'd been alive, but it seemed that after he'd passed away, I'd spent a lot of my time alone.

Eden hurried toward the courtyard with Toby, his leash, her list, and her cell phone, and I'd just sat down to go over my to-do list when an incoming call from Hazel came through. Since I'd just spoken to her, I was surprised to see that the call was from her.

"Is everything okay?" I asked.

"Everything is fine. I'm with Lily, and she asked me if I could help her with her mother's car. The police have released it, and Lily has an interested buyer. She hoped I would pick it up from the impound lot and then meet the buyer, but I'll need someone to follow me and bring me home once I drop the vehicle off."

I wrinkled my nose. "Someone bought that car?"

"Apparently. So can you help me out, or should I call Velma? Lily really doesn't want to ever see the car again."

"I can help you. I'll pick you up at your house, and then we'll head to the impound lot. I assume that Lily arranged for us to pick the vehicle up."

"She did. In fact, Alex said that she'd meet us there to make sure we don't encounter any problems."

As promised, Alex met Hazel and me at the impound lot. It wasn't as if Gwen's death had been bloody, so the car was in good shape. I wouldn't personally want to drive a car someone had died in, but Lily was selling it at a deep discount, and I supposed some folks didn't mind who'd owned the car or what happened in it before they bought it.

"I have something you might be interested in." Alex held up an envelope.

"What is it?" Hazel asked.

"The car registration, a copy of the insurance card, and similar items. I didn't go through all the paperwork when the car was towed in, but I decided to look at everything closer now that the car was being released, and I found this."

She handed Hazel a single sheet of paper. Hazel paled.

"What is it?" I asked.

"A suicide note," Hazel answered.

I gasped.

Hazel finished reading the sheet of paper and then handed it to me. "I really did think that our theory that Gwen had just gotten into her car, started the engine, and then forgot what she was doing was a good one, but based on this note, it looks as if Gwen actually did do what I'd been so sure she never would," Hazel said.

I read the note. In it, Gwen explaincd that she was simply too distraught to go on living without Calvin, and she hoped everyone would forgive her for taking the easy way out.

"I don't think Gwen wrote this note," I said.

"What do you mean that Gwen didn't write it? Who else would have written it?" Alex asked.

"Wanda Anderson." I turned the page around so that the text was facing Alex. "Bright green ink."

Alex looked confused.

"Wanda came into the bookstore the other day to pick up some special-order books. She wrote me a check with a logo pen from a bookstore located about an hour down the coast. The pen featured bright green ink… ink that was the exact color as the ink used to write this suicide note."

Alex paused and then responded. "I suppose that might seem significant, but if the pen used by Wanda was a logo pen from a bookstore, which is only about sixty miles down the coast, then it stands to reason that Gwen may have had the exact same pen."

I turned the page around and took a closer look. "I may be wrong, and you make a good point about other locals having the same pen, but Wanda added a loop to her W in an exceptionally unique way." I pointed to a 'W' on the suicide note. "Just like this."

Alex took the suicide note from me and took a few moments to study it, then asked if I still had the check Wanda had given me. I didn't, but I was sure the bank had a copy on file. Alex agreed that was likely and called the bank. They emailed a copy of the check to her, which she used to confirm that the suicide note found in Gwen Harbinger's car had very likely been written by Wanda Anderson.

I looked at Hazel. "I really am so very sorry. I know you were friends with both Gwen and Calvin."

Hazel looked a lot paler than she had just a few minutes ago. "What do we do now?" she asked Alex.

"It looks as if I need to have a conversation with Wanda."

"We should go with you," Hazel said.

"No," Alex responded. "I appreciate your help." She glanced at me. "Both of you. But this is official police business. I really need to take care of this on my own. Cooper is with Gabby so I'll call her to let her know what is going on and then I'll head over now."

Hazel looked as if she was going to pass out, so I promised Alex I'd make sure Hazel got home okay. The poor woman appeared to be in shock, which I certainly understood. While Alex and I were new to the community, Hazel had lived here for a long time and had known Gwen, Calvin, and Wanda. I knew Hazel would be okay once she'd had a chance to process everything, but the tragic and needless deaths of two longtime residents would leave a cloud hanging over the town for quite some time.

Chapter 17

It had been three weeks since Alex confronted and then arrested Wanda. Wanda admitted that while she'd suspected her husband had been having an affair for a while, she'd had no idea who the affair might have been with. When Wanda found a note in Desi's pocket that suggested he'd been sneaking out to meet Gwen, Wanda went to Gwen's house, intent on confronting her. When she arrived at Gwen's house, she found a half-empty pitcher of iced tea on the table. Initially, Wanda hadn't seen Gwen and had all but decided that Gwen wasn't home, but Wanda decided to check the garage for her car at the last minute. She found Gwen sitting in the car inside the closed-up garage, staring into space. Wanda admitted that Gwen seemed totally out of it, either not talking at all or talking nonsense when she did speak. Wanda suspected that Gwen was on drugs, really, really potent drugs. While she initially only planned to talk to the woman she suspected of ruining her marriage, when Wanda found Gwen sitting in her car inside the closed garage, she acted on impulse.

Wanda found a piece of paper, wrote a simple suicide note, put the note on the seat next to Gwen, started the engine, and left. She knew that it was possible Gwen might come to her senses and save herself before she died of carbon monoxide poisoning, but Wanda also admitted that she couldn't bear to watch Gwen die, so she'd decided to let happen what would happen.

What stood out in my mind was that Wanda had told Alex that she had put the suicide note on the seat next to Gwen, while Alex had said that she found the note in the envelope with the registration and insurance information. The only conclusion we could agree on was that at some point before she died, Gwen must have noticed the piece of paper and believed it was something that belonged with the other paperwork in the glove box and slipped it inside the envelope. If that wasn't what happened, then I was afraid we'd have another mystery that would likely never be solved.

It had taken a while, but Lily's older brother, David, had finally shown up. The man didn't have a lot of time to commit to working out the details in Holiday Bay, but between the two of them, Lily and David had managed to cremate their mother and then spread her ashes, along with their father's ashes, from the bow of their father's boat. Calvin's crew had helped with the small ceremony, and once that was done, David had signed the vessel over to his father's crew members in lieu of back wages owed. Once that was accomplished, he put the house up for sale and headed home to his job and fiancée.

Lily had taken a little more time to settle on a plan, but she'd eventually decided to return to school. The entire experience had sobered her, and I suspected it had encouraged her to grow up a bit. The youngest son had never shown up, but Lily and David reported that Martin not showing was exactly the sort of thing he'd do, and neither seemed worried about it, so I decided I wouldn't worry either.

"I'm excited about tonight's book club meeting," I said to Velma as she worked on arranging her supplies in the cupboards above the coffee and pastry bar. "The completion of the remodel took a bit longer than planned, but everything came out just perfect. I'm excited for everyone to see what we've accomplished."

"I really do love the way the colors and textures all came together," Velma said. "I wasn't sure in the beginning if running a coffee and pastry bar would even be something I was interested in, but I've really enjoyed working with you, and having the opportunity to work in a freshly remodeled space is like the frosting on the cake. Is Hazel going to bring the first rescues by today?"

I nodded. "Yes, Hazel's bringing a mama cat and six kittens today. The mama and her babies have been living in a foster home and are ready for their forever homes. Hazel has assured me that they're adorable and should find forever homes quickly."

"So, how exactly is this supposed to work?" Eden, who'd been dusting shelves, asked.

"If someone is interested in adopting one of the cats we're showcasing, we have them fill out an application. Each cat is wearing a collar, and each collar has a number on it. We just need to put the number of the cat or kitten the prospective adopter is interested in on the paperwork and then fax the whole thing to Hazel. She'll process the application, and if approved, she'll come by and pick the feline up and then she'll deliver him or her to their new home."

"That sounds simple enough," Velma said.

"Yeah," Eden agreed. "But I imagine I'll miss the kittens when they're gone."

"Hazel will bring new cats to us as they are adopted, so it won't be like we'll be suffering from the effect of an empty house," I assured her.

"Maybe you can get a kitten of your own once you find an apartment," Velma suggested to Eden.

"Actually," Eden said. "I found an apartment. A small studio opened up in Nikki's building. It really is tiny. No bigger than a motel room, but it has a mini fridge and microwave, and more importantly, I can afford it. It'll be a good place to start. Once I save some money, I can look for something larger. Unfortunately, they don't allow pets, but that's okay since I don't really have time to be a full-time pet parent right now. Once I'm more established and have a larger place, I'll look into adopting a pet."

I agreed that sounded like a good plan, and then I headed upstairs to check on the progress being made on my apartment. The remodel of the second floor and the attic would take quite a bit longer to complete than the remodel of the first floor had taken. Lonnie indicated that I should be able to move in by the end of September or possibly the beginning of October. I hoped he'd be finished with the remodel in plenty of time for me to get all moved in before the first-ever Halloween event Velma and I planned to sponsor as co-owners got underway. We'd been discussing options for the event, but with everything that was going on, we decided to start small. Eden had suggested we bring in a guest author from the horror genre. After discussing various options, we decided on a different author each week during October, probably on Tuesdays or Thursdays, who might be interested in discussing a Halloween-themed book regardless of genre.

On another positive note, the engineer had approved all the windows I wanted to add to the space upstairs. The fact that the building was brick made it tougher to make the additions, but overall, the structure was a lot sturdier than a wooden structure would have been. The windows would need to be specially ordered to fit our measurements, but Lonnie assured me he'd take care of ordering them right away, and they should be delivered in plenty of time to get everything done by the deadline he'd set for himself.

Once I'd climbed the steep staircase to the second floor, I took a few moments to look around. Creating a loft and putting the bedroom in the attic space would allow me to have a much larger living area. Lonnie had mapped out a living space featuring a single large room with a smallish kitchen divided by a dining counter. The main bathroom had a shower and a tub, and in addition to the larger bathroom downstairs, I had a small closet bathroom with only a toilet and sink in the loft. Once the windows were installed, the view would be stunning. I really couldn't wait to see how it all came together. I'd spent a fair amount of time imagining my life in my own little corner of the world. Toby and I would enjoy curling up by the gas fireplace to watch the storms roll in from the sea. There just seemed to be something about sitting high up on a perch looking down on the rest of the world that added to the cozy feel.

During these quiet moments when I was alone with my thoughts, I couldn't help but think about how great it would have been if Gus had been around to join me in my little eagle nest in the sky. Of course, dwelling on what could never be wasn't the best way to spend my time, but now and then, I couldn't help but wonder.

Shaking the cobwebs from my mind, I was about to head downstairs when Velma could be heard coming up the stairs.

"You left your cell phone on the counter near the cash register," Velma informed me. "I heard it ring, so I looked at the caller ID. It was Tuck."

I raised a brow.

"I wasn't sure if you'd want to call him back right away, but I figured I should let you know that he called and then let you decide."

I held my hand out and took the cell phone. "Thank you. I appreciate the heads up."

She smiled and nodded and then headed back down the stairs.

I knew that Velma had experienced a similar situation with Royce when they'd first run into each other on Nantucket Island. He'd been a blast from her past that she hadn't been sure she'd wanted to reacquaint herself with, but Royce had been the persistent sort, and she'd eventually given in and agreed to go out with him. In their case, his insistence led to happily ever after. Somehow, I didn't see that in the cards for Tuck and me. The guilt I'd feel every time I was with the man I'd once loved would be too much to deal with, and in the end, I was pretty sure I'd end up sending Tuck away as I had forty years ago. No, I decided, it was best to let him down now. I'd listen to the message and call him back, but once I had him on the line, I'd very firmly tell him that I wasn't interested in exploring whatever it was he might be offering.

I felt confident that my plan was a good one. I listened to Tuck's message, expecting it to contain an invitation to get together. Instead, he'd called to let me know that he was at the airport and heading overseas. He stumbled around a bit and admitted that he hadn't initially planned to fill me in on his plans since I'd never gotten back to him after his previous call. Then, when his plane had been delayed, he had time to think about things. After an hour touring the highlights from his trip down memory lane, he'd remembered why he'd loved me and felt it would be prudent to try again. He went on to say he just wanted to talk and assured me there was no pressure to commit to being anything other than friends. He reminded me that we'd once been great friends and that he felt confident we could go there again. He closed by informing me that he'd be away for a month or possibly six weeks. He said he'd miss me and promised to call me when he got back into town to set something up.

At that moment, part of me wanted to call and tell him not to bother to call, while another part wanted to call him and tell him that I'd never stopped thinking about him. I'd loved Tuck once, and in some ways, I supposed I still did, but Gus and Tuck had been bitter rivals, and I knew that if I opened even a small door for Tuck, I'd be betraying the man I'd been wed to for more than forty years. The man I still loved. The man I would always love.

I'd actually thought a lot about how my life would play out from this point forward. I knew that with the exception of Tuck, Gus wouldn't begrudge me a second love, but I'd also concluded that love was something you did when you were young. An uncomplicated life with my kitten and new friends for company really did seem a better path than the rocky one leading to romance.

Slipping my cell phone into my pocket, I headed back downstairs. Calling Tuck could wait.

"The Halloween decorations we ordered are here," Eden said with enthusiasm as she opened boxes and began stacking their contents on the long counter at the front of the store. She sat back on her heels. "Can you believe that summer is nearly over?"

"I can't," I agreed. "But there is a hint of a chill in the air, and the leaves in the higher elevations are already beginning to turn. Before you know it, we'll be planning for snow."

Velma groaned at the mention of snow while Eden expressed her enthusiasm for all that a snowy season had to offer. Being the sort who'd always enjoyed the first snow of the season, I had to admit that I agreed with Eden when it came to my anticipation for the frozen white stuff.

"This will be the first Halloween I'm going to actually be able to enjoy in a long time," Eden said. She laughed. "Last year, I was living in a real house of horrors. I'm hoping for a fun and spooky drama-free holiday this year."

I wanted to ask about her comment about the "real house of horrors" but decided it could wait. I had a feeling that going too fast with the background inquiries I was dying to ask my new employee might send her running.

"Haven told me that they're having a lot of fun events out at the inn. A harvest festival, a haunted hayride, and a murder mystery dinner, to name a few. A few events are just for guests, but most are open to the general public. It would be fun to try to go to a few things."

"It would be," I agreed. "We had a haunted hayride-type event back in my hometown in Minnesota when I lived there. Gus and I tried to go every year."

"Did you dress up?" she asked.

"Actually, we did." I smiled as I thought back to the year Gus and I had dressed as Sonny and Cher. "Maybe the Sonny and Cher costumes weren't as scary as they could have been, but we'd looked awesome and had a lot of fun."

"Who are Sonny and Cher?" Eden asked.

I glanced at Velma, and she smiled. Sometimes I really did feel old.

"I guess I'll head to the backroom and set up the chairs," Velma offered.

The room we used for the book club meetings had been painted and re-carpeted during the remodel. The view out the window was as good as it had ever been, but now there were lights accenting the window that made the whole thing seem even brighter. Tonight's book was a mystery that took place in a purportedly haunted house. It might have been a better selection for October, but when Shelby had suggested it, and Marnie and Alice had whole-heartedly agreed, I knew the book was likely worth the time it would take to read. And it had been. In fact, it had been one of the best books I'd read in a long time.

By the time Velma returned from setting up the chairs for the meeting, Marnie and Cricket had arrived with the Singleton sisters. Shortly after they glided in, Shelby arrived with Georgia, Emma, and Savannah, and then Nikki arrived with Haven, who made a beeline toward Eden. I knew that an additional fifteen to twenty women would show up ready to discuss the juiciest topics of the hour within the next fifteen minutes. Some would have read the book we'd chosen as our weekly selection, while others would claim they'd never gotten around to it.

I supposed that it really didn't matter. We were a book club of the soul. It was true that books were discussed to an extent, but the real reason the woman who attended the Tuesday night book club meeting showed up week after week had more to do with the community we'd cultivated rather than the books we would read.

We were an eclectic group representing a wide-spread range of backgrounds, ages, education, and social status. While it would have been easy to dissect our differences and pin them to a board for all to see, we were all the same in many ways. Each and every one of us, regardless of age or financial position, had a deep-seated love for our community, an understanding of the true value of friendship, a hunger for a lively discussion, and a commitment to the sort of kinship that must be planted and nurtured over time.

USA Today best-selling author Kathi Daley lives in beautiful Lake Tahoe with her husband, Ken. When she isn't writing, she likes spending time hiking the miles of desolate trails surrounding her home. Find out more about her books at www.kathidaley.com